TORMENTED BY THE KING

THE MURDOCH MAFIA SERIES
BOOK 2

SAMANTHA BARRETT

To all the bad girls out there that can bring a bad boy to his knees,
This one is for you, my Queens.

AUTHORS NOTE

This book may make some uncomfortable with the content.
I have always sworn if I ever wrote Mafia book, I would go
dark,
in order to stay true to my character's that is what I have
done.
Some scenes and descriptions may make you uneasy,
make you feel squeamish but rest assured there is a HEA.
For those who have read my PNR and thought they were
dark, well this is worse, so much worse but in the best way
possible.

Welcome to the Murdoch Mafia and all their fucked up
shit.

Chapter One

King

I can't stand to be around him. He hid the truth from me!

I've stood by his side through everything. Even when he killed our father, I never, not even once, doubted him. I've had his back through all the backlash, through all the uproar our father's death caused. I've never gone against him, until now. I drive around aimlessly. I don't even know where the fuck I'm going, I just know I can't go home right now or I'll kill him.

He's so fucking caught up in eating Kiara's cunt he can't see straight. I love Kiara, I really do, but her pussy is blinding him and we are paying the cost. He eliminated the Ramano family tonight and didn't even tell us. He took out one of the five fucking founding families and doesn't think he needs to tell us. This doesn't only impact him, it affects all of us. Our sister ran and he hasn't done anything to fucking find her. She was kidnapped, then takes off and he acts like it's fine!

Nothing is fucking fine, it hasn't been for three years. My brothers are struggling. Knight has shut us all out and no one except Bishop knows why. Rook hides behind his humor but I can see darkness inside him. It should be Bishop who is looking out for them, not me! I'm not their father. Tony was a piece of shit and I don't miss the fucker but since he's been gone the twins have spiraled. Carlina has retreated inside herself, Bishop has focused more running the mafia empire Tony built instead of helping raise our siblings. I was the one who held the twins through their tears. They don't know what Tony did to Car or Kiara, I told them Bishop killed him but not the reason why. They trust me enough to know B wouldn't have taken him out unless he had a fucking epic reason why. My phone rings through the Bluetooth in the car. Luka's name pops up. Sighing I hit answer on the steering wheel.

"What?" I snap.

"Take your next left." I white knuckle the steering wheel and grit my teeth in anger.

"The fuck, Luka?" I growl.

"Trust me, I'm helping you when I shouldn't." That piques my curiosity. I take the next left like he instructed and wait for his next instructions. I follow his directions until I end up at a set of wrought iron gates.

"Where the fuck did you take me?"

"They open at eight tomorrow morning. Put two and two together, King." I read the sign on the gate and deflate, my stomach sinks.

Pac Pines Cemetery.

"This is where she is?" I whisper. Luka may work for Bishop but he and I are close. Him giving me this information would warrant Bishop putting a bullet in his head. Mav would never go against Bishop's order like this. He and I may be friends but his loyalty to Bish is strong as fuck.

"Yeah bro, she's there. They have cameras. I can hack them but I don't want the bad juju." I chuckle despite my sour mood. Luka is a fucking pussy when it comes to disturbing the dead as he puts it. "I'll catch ya later."

"Luka?" He sighs.

"Don't mention it. You would do the same for me."

"You know I would." I mean it, I would take a bullet for Luka. That guy has saved my ass ten times over from being full of lead.

"He's out looking for you," he hedges. I shake my head even though he can't see me.

"I don't care. He lied to me!"

"He had his reasons. Hear him out." I glare at the screen on my dash.

"You knew?" There's a long pause before he answers.

"It's my job to know."

"Right." I end the call and smack my head a few times against the headrest angry at... everyone. They fucking lied. I gave her up for them, to protect my family so I could focus on them and help takeover from Tony. I gave her up, now I'll have to live with the regret of my choice for the rest of my life.

The sun beaming on my face has me groaning and opening my eyes. I look around and realize I must have fallen asleep outside the gates of the cemetery. I sit forward and hop out of my car stretching, my fucking back and neck is stiff as shit from sleeping in the car. I pull my phone from my pocket and check the time, it's nearly eight. A war of emotions swirls inside me.

Do I go in?

Do I just leave?

Before I can debate on the matter any longer, I watch as someone walks toward the gates from the other side. He eyes me warily but says nothing as he begins to unlock the chain and lock around the gates and opens them for the day. I stand frozen for a beat until he turns to walk away but I call out stopping him.

"Yeah?" He runs his gaze over me clearly unsure of me and I don't blame him. I have blood all over from my fight with Bishop and must look like a state. I run a hand through my hair and pluck up the courage to ask.

"Can you help me find someone?" His face contorts with confusion but he nods.

"Who you looking for?" I take a deep breath and say the name I haven't said aloud in a long time.

"Christine Vaughn?" He nods and motions for me to follow him. I grab my keys and kick the door closed as I run after him. I pull my shirt out making sure it's covering the gun in the back of my waistband. We walk for a few minutes until a small pokey office comes into view. I wait outside as he heads in—there isn't enough room in there for the both of us, it reminds me of a toll booth. He pokes his head out the door band narrows his eyes at me.

"You family?" A whoosh of air escapes me as I answer his question.

"I'm her... kid's father." Hearing those words come from my own mouth has something inside me constricting. I have a fucking kid! I shake my head and decide to reflect on that bit of information later on, right now I need to deal with this before going after my little girl. He nods and comes out motioning for me to follow him. I do. We pass by so many graves. Most people would be feeling some type of way about being here but death doesn't scare me. It's inevitable. We all die—it's not a matter of if, it's a matter of when. He leads me toward a massive tree where there are many head-stones and motions to the one on the end of the six that are nestled in the shade of the tree. I nod my thanks as he turns and leaves me. I stand here stock still, just staring.

Just fucking get it over with, King! I berate myself as I move slowly toward her grave... toward the woman I loved.

Christine and I were toxic together, there is no denying that, but as much as we fought, we fucked harder. I still loved her regardless. My family hated her. They can try to say otherwise but the looks in their eyes told me all I needed to know. She would never be accepted in my family as one of us, like Kiara. I rest my hand atop her stone and feel a lump form in my throat at the sight of her name.

Christine Vaughn
Beloved, mother, daughter, sister and friend.
May the angels rejoice in her presence.

I grind my teeth together in anger, I don't even fucking know how she died!

A deep churning in my gut tells me my family had something to do with her death. I crouch down and run my fingers over her name.

"I promise I will find our daughter. I'll raise her like you would have wanted and love her with everything that I am. I'm so sorry... I wasn't there. I vow to you that I'll never rest until I avenge you, Christine." With that said I stand and leave. I have every intention of going after my daughter and bringing her home with me but first, I need to change and sort shit with Bishop because that bastard owes me an explanation. It better be a good one or he'll be buried beside Tony in an unmarked grave!

Chapter Two

Allison

"Wake up!" I smile and haul the blankets over my head keeping my eyes closed.

"Five more minutes!" I beg. I have no idea how this kid has so much damn energy at this early hour.

"I neeeed pancakes!" I smile and open my eyes as I lower the blankets and stare at the most beautiful little girl I have ever seen in my life. Her pout has me laughing and reaching out to tickle her. She squeals and tries to escape my reach but I hold firm. "Sowiii."

"Do you give up?"

"Yessss," she squeals out through her laughter.

"What's the word?" I laugh.

"Mercy." I stop tickling her. She launches forward and wraps her arms around my neck as she tackles me back down. I hold her close and breath in her strawberry conditioner. Just the feeling of her hug has a pang of sadness thrumming through me. Christine should be here, this should be her moment with Mela, not mine.

"Come on then, let's get you some pancakes, then we have to get you ready for school." She pulls back and frowns at me.

"I don't like it." I deflate as I reach out and tuck her brown hair that hints of blonde through it behind her ear. I look into her green eyes and I know they are her father's. Christine had blue eyes like me. I've only ever seen one picture of King—Amelia looks exactly like her father.

"I know, baby girl. I wish you didn't have to go but Ally has to go to work or we can't get more pancakes." A sad look clouds her features as she nods. I hate that I can't give her everything that she wants—being a single mom is fucking hard. I make sure all her needs are met though. She may not have everything she wants but I make sure as hell that she has everything she needs.

***

I'm just finishing cleaning up our dishes when Mela walks into the kitchen, changed and ready for her day at kindergarten. I smile down at her.

"Did you brush your teeth?" She nods eagerly.

"Yep."

"Okay, let's go." I wipe my hands on the cloth, grab my purse and Mela's bag as we head for the door. Every morning when we leave I always feel like I'm being watched. I shiver at the thought as we make our way down the stairs of our apartment building and push open the main door. The sun is beaming down and a warm breeze wraps around me like a blanket. Amelia grips my hand and I smile down at her as we walk the short distance to her school. I can't shake the feeling that we're being followed. I keep looking over my shoulder and darting my gaze side to side.

"Can we get ice cream?" I smile down at her.

"Yes, we can get ice cream after I pick you up." She beams up me and skips along beside me. I feel her grip tighten on my hand as her school comes into view. I hate that I have to send her away daily but it's not like her mother had life insurance or anything. I had to drop out of college to raise her and get a full-time job that I fucking hate. My boss is a sleezy fucker and makes passes at me daily. Sarah, the head teacher, smiles at us as we walk through the door.

"Morning, Miss Amelia." Mela smiles shyly up at her. I crouch down in front of her and smile reassuringly.

"I tell you what. You be a good girl today and no tears, we'll get ice cream after I pick you up and we can watch movies till late tonight." Her face morphs into pure happiness. She nods eagerly and places a quick kiss on my cheek before grabbing her bag and following after Sarah. My heart bursts with love, that kid has no idea how much she has changed my life and given it a purpose. I check my watch and curse, I'm gonna be late.

I burst through the front door and shoot Sally an apologetic smile. She shoots me a look telling me Kevin is pissed that I'm five minutes late. I dart in the back, put my bag away, and come out the front and tie my apron around my waist, then slide up next to Sally at the till.

"How pissed is he?" I whisper.

"On a war path," is all she manages to get out before he calls for me. I cringe when customers turn their gazes to me. I trudge slowly into the back past the kitchen to Kevin's dirty little office. He stands behind his desk with the bottom of his stomach resting on top. I mean, couldn't he at least wear a shirt that covers his whole gut and not have the bottom hanging out? His balding head gleams under the exposed light, brown eyes filled with lust as he scans them over me. I fight the gag that wants to break through at the thought of him mentally undressing me. His ginger mustache curled at the ends—his breaths sound like someone is breathing into a paper bag. The man is severely overweight.

"I'm sorry I was late, Mela–"

"Don't make excuses. Get that kid sorted earlier in the mornings. I don't pay you to be late." I fight the angry remark that wants to tear out of me at the way he speaks about Mela.

"Yes, sir. It won't happen again." The tension flees his body as his gaze drops to my ample chest causing me to cringe in disgust.

"You know, if you would like, I could take you to dinner and we could discuss boarding schools for her?" I clench my hands into fists at my sides.

"She's four years old," I grit out through clenched teeth. He shrugs and waves me off.

"Still, I'm sure there's some out there that take the sprogs at that age." It takes everything inside me to not tell him to go fuck himself. If I didn't need this job so badly I would have quit months ago, but I have bills to pay. Like a good girl I smile and fucking thank the disgusting pig for the offer before going back out front to help Sally take orders. I will my tears back down. I hate that I have to take his shit.

Christine never had a fucking will or anything in place and my only saving grace was she never named the father on the birth certificate. I don't legally have guardianship of Mela, though to everyone that knows her they all think she is my kid. It's nearly the end of my shift and my feet are killing me, my hair reeks of grease and my back is aching from bending all day. I head over to the corner booth where a man sits, I don't even look at him to ask for his order.

"What can I get you?"

"My kid." The anger in his tone has me looking up from my pad. He's wearing a ball cap low over his head and a pair of sunglasses that conceal his eyes from me.

"Excuse me?" Surely, I must have heard him wrong. It's been a long as fuck day and I just want to pick my girl up and go home. He reaches up and removes his cap, his brown hair with flecks of blond is plastered back against his head, he grips the edges of his glasses and slowly lifts them. A feeling of dread settles inside me, something bad is about to happen... I can feel it. When he places the glasses atop his head and I see his eyes I drop my pad and pen. Green eyes that I know so very well stare back at me. Unlike the loving eyes I'm used to seeing, his hold so much hatred and anger inside them. I stumble back a step and shake my head. He darts out of the booth so quickly for a man his size and grips my arms holding me in place. I stare up at him open mouthed. I can feel other patrons gazes on us but I'm too caught up in him to even care.

"I want my kid, Allison." A cold shiver rushes through me. He knows my name, he knows about her. Tears prick the corners of my eyes as I shake my head unable to get my voice to work.

"You gonna have to unhand her now, sir!" He snaps his gaze over my head to look at Sally. She may be old and fragile but let me tell you, Sally is from the south and that woman doesn't take no shit from anybody!

"Stay out of this," he hisses.

"Nah-uh. You just go on ahead now and release Miss Ally and get on out of here." He pulls his gaze from her to focus back on me, so many emotions in his eyes but the most dominant one is hatred. It sends a shiver down my spine.

"I want to see her, Allison. You have till tomorrow to make contact or I'll be here again and next time, I won't be leaving without my daughter." He releases me with a hard shove. I smack into the table behind me and grip the edge so I don't fall. He reaches into his pocket and I freeze, waiting for him to draw his gun and shoot me where I stand for daring to take his child from him. I know exactly who he and his family are. I will never allow him to pull my niece into his lifestyle and corrupt her like he did my sister! He pulls a card out and closes the space between us before slamming the card down beside me, causing me to jump. He leans down until I feel his lips brush against the shell of my ear, causing my body to react in a way it shouldn't. "Don't fuck me around. You won't like what happens if you do." I nod like an idiot. He pulls back and shoots one last scathing look at me before turning and storming out of the diner. I slump forward and gasp for air as soon as the door slams closed behind him. Sally rushes over and rubs her hand up and down my back.

"You okay?" I nod. "You know who he is?" I nod. She releases a disproving sigh which has me standing up straight to face her. "It's not my business who you spend your time with. I don't need to tell you that he isn't a good man to have around young Amelia."

"He's her father," I whisper.

Chapter Three

Allison

After getting ripped a new asshole from Kevin I clocked out and picked Mela up, stopping to get ice cream on our way home. We're cuddled up on the couch with her sleeping next to me with her head in my lap. I run my fingers through her hair and war with myself. I don't believe his threat was empty. I know he meant what he said, I could see it in his eyes. If I don't call, I know he will come back. But if I call him, I can maybe make this work in my favor. I ponder it for a few minutes before gently sliding out from under Mela, not wanting to wake her. I pull the throw blanket over her and take a deep breath. I always knew it would be a possibility that he would find out about her but I just thought I had more time to... figure things out by then, I guess.

I grab his card from my purse. All it says is King Murdoch and his number. I try to talk myself into it, just get this phone call over with but I'm scared. He has the money and resources to take Mela from me and he has every right to do that, she's his kid. The thought of losing her has an ache forming in my chest and a lump rising in my throat. I can't let that happen! I dial the number and don't even think as I push call. It rings three times before he answers.

"Yeah?" I open my mouth but words fail me—what the hell do I even say? "Who the fuck is this?" His angry tone has me snapping out of my stupor.

"I-it's Allison." I hate that I sound so meek. There's a slight pause before he speaks again.

"I expected to be intercepting you at the airport." I recoil, shocked he would think such a thing.

"Why would I be at an airport?"

"Running with my daughter like you have been for years!" That has my anger spiking. He has no fucking idea what I have been through these past four years raising Mela on my own. What I've given up to give her the best life I can.

"I haven't run anywhere. I've been right fucking here!" I hear something smash on the other end that causes me to flinch. I refuse to allow him to bully me into thinking I did something wrong. I did what was best for Amelia and I don't fucking regret it.

"Yeah, hiding my fucking kid from me!" he roars.

"I didn't hide her, that was Christine's choice to make, not mine!" I snap back. I quickly head to my room not wanting to wake Mela up with my raised voice.

"Bullshit. I had every right to know I had a fucking kid. You and your sister decided to keep it from me. I want my daughter, Allison," I snap. I will not sit here and allow him to demand things of me.

"You will not take her from me!" I'm so proud of how my voice doesn't waiver and how strong I sound, when inside I feel like I'm a shivering mess and he isn't even in front of me.

"I'll do whatever the fuck I want."

"She needs me." He's silent for a beat and my heart thuds in my chest.

"You have three days, Allison."

"T-three days for what?"

"To spend time with her before I come for my daughter." I stop breathing, tears cloud my vision. "You try to run... I'll stop you. You think of trying anything stupid with her and it will be the last thing you ever do." I place my hand over my mouth to muffle my sob. My worst fear is coming to life and I can't handle it.

"P-please, don't do this, she needs me," I beg. I don't have the money to board a plane or even drive away with her. I don't own a fucking car. I had to sell it to get the down payment for this apartment.

"It's already been done. Three days is all you get." He ends the call and I crumple to my knees as sobs wreck my body. I try to muffle them behind my hand and quiet myself down so Mela doesn't hear me breaking apart. He has no idea what she likes, how she falls asleep, which is her favorite teddy... He knows nothing about her. She has asthma. If she has an attack would he know what to do then? I don't know what I'm going to do but I know I can't just roll over and allow him to come and try take her from me.

Three days later...

My time is up. Mela and I round the corner toward our run-down apartment building and the blacked-out Range Rover that is parked in front of our building sticks out like a sore thumb. A lump forms in my throat as I slam to a stop. Mela pauses beside me. I can feel her gaze on me but I can't look at her, instead I just reach down and scoop her up in my arms and carry her the rest of the way. When we are close enough, the door opens and he steps out. He's dressed casual like the other day—dark wash jeans, a blue polo shirt but no hat. He glares at me as I walk past and mutter,

"The park." I don't stop to see if he's following. There is a run-down park across the street that has a set of swings, a slide and couple other things. I avoid coming here but since King is with us, I figure it will be safe enough for Mela to have a play whilst I try talk some sense into her... father. I stop near the slide and place her on her feet crouching down in front of her. I help her remove her pack. She beams at me and I return her smile, her little brows furrow as she looks up to the shadow that looms above me. She leans in closer and try as she might this girl cannot whisper to save her life.

"There is a pretty man behind you, Ally." I chuckle. King snorts trying to mask his laugh behind me. I grin at my smart beautiful girl and speak.

"Why don't you go play for a bit while I talk to... him." I can feel his disapproving stare on me but I don't give a shit. She nods eagerly and heads over to the slide. As I slowly stand to my feet I can the feel heat radiating off of him against my back, he's so close to me that only a sliver of space remains between us. I take a deep breath and steel my spine as I slowly turn to face him. He's too close so I have to step back and crane my neck up to look into his eyes. He isn't focused on me, his gaze is zeroed in on the little girl that is a mirror image of him. "Please don't take her from me." I speak low enough so that Mela won't be able to overhear us. He slowly pulls his gaze from her. It seems almost painful for him to not be able to watch her and focus on me. His eyes shine with hatred as he peers down at me. A part of me doesn't blame him for how he feels but another part of me hates him too, for what he put my sister through.

"She belongs with me." I shake my head denying his claim.

"No, she belongs with someone who loves her." His upper lip pulls back in a snarl as he closes the space between us trying to use his height and size to intimidate me. I won't lie, it works. He is freaking huge, the size of his body dwarfs my own. His arms are bigger than my thigh and I felt his hands on me, they are big enough to wrap around my neck and squeeze the life from me.

"You and your sister never gave me the chance to love my own kid!" I drop my gaze unable to hold his stare any longer. I nod my head defeated and turn to watch my girl. Looking at her and watching her smile is like a drug for me, I crave it daily. The only way to explain how I feel for Mela is like watching my own heart exist outside of my body.

"Ally, Ally, look at me."

"I'm watching, baby girl," I call back. I can hear the watery tone of my own voice and fight back the tears as I watch her go down the slide. I bite my lip to stop it from trembling, I have to woman up and do this. I turn back to him, shocked to find his gaze on me and not Amelia. "Her name is Amelia. She is four years old and loves unicorns." My voice aches and the tears I have fought begin to fall as I tell him all about my baby girl. "She loves bubble baths and can only have them as a treat if she eats her veggies at dinner. She doesn't like to wash her hair daily, only every second night. She still sucks her thumb whenever she goes to sleep and will only sleep if she has Mr. Snaggles. She won't fall asleep in her own room–" He cuts me off.

"Why are you telling me all of this?" I sniffle and dry my eyes with the backs of my hands but the tears keep coming.

"You need to know this stuff if you plan to take her from me. She needs the comforts that she is used–"

"You think I can't buy her everything that she needs and wants?" I flinch at the reminder that he is indeed able to supply her with everything her heart would desire, unlike me.

"It's not about money," I grit out. "She doesn't give a shit about what you can buy her, she isn't that type of kid. She loves quality time and being held while you watch a movie. She loves hugs on the couch and being with you, not left alone in her room with a fucking iPad!" I'm so angry I can't even look at him so I turn away and watch Mela. When I see her trying to hop on the swings and failing, I grab my purse and storm over to her. She smiles up at me, which I can't muster the strength to return and I feel like a bitch. Instead, I offer to help her on and buckle her into the child's swing as I push her. I try to block the conversation with King from my mind as I focus on Mela and her laughter. Just the sound of it has my anger bleeding away and my hurt returning. I'm gonna have to say goodbye to her and I don't fucking know how to do that. I stop the swing and help her off, ignoring her protests. I scoop her and our bags up and march past King.

He follows us the whole way up the stairs and stands behind me as I unlock the door and push it open. The petty bitch inside me wants to kick it closed so it smacks him in the face but then another part of me also knows he probably has a gun on him and I don't want to get shot in front of Mela. I stop in the living and turn to face King. He eyes me skeptically but I don't give a shit.

"Mela's room is down the hall second on the left, you can wait in there while I speak with her... please." It takes a moment but he eventually nods and does as I ask. I pop Mela on the couch and sit on the small table in front of her, trying to build the courage I need to tell her that I can't be with her anymore. My fucking heart is shattering inside my chest at the thought of living my life without her. I will never recover from her loss.

Chapter Four

King

I look around her small room. She has a small single bed in the corner with some pink netting thing that hangs from the roof surrounding the bed. She has fucking hundreds of soft toys scattered around her room and photos of unicorns hung on the walls. I spot some framed pictures near her bed and make my way over. I pick up the one closest to me, it's a photo of Allison and Amelia on her 1st birthday. Allison's blonde hair was longer, unlike her pixie cut now, her blue eyes shine with so much love as she gazes down at my little girl. I return that frame and grab the next. It's another one of Allison and Amelia in a small child's pool, both of them are beaming in happiness at the camera. My anger roars to life inside me—she stole years from me. I could have been there for all those birthdays but Allison kept her from me! I pick up the last photo and can only stand to look at it for a few seconds, Allison has her hands on Christine's pregnant belly, both of them smiling at the camera. Allison's eyes shine with love, while her sisters, they have something sinister lurking beneath the surface.

"No! I won't." At the sound of Amelia's shout, I drop the photo on her bed and rush out to the living room. Allison has tears streaking down her cheeks as she looks to my daughter.

"Please, Mela, I don't want you to go either but–"

"Ally, no." At the anguish tone of her voice something inside me stills, I never want to hear that tone come from my daughter again. "I want to live with you. I be good, I promise. No more cream and no more bad at schools." Allison sobs as she reaches out for Amelia and yanks her into her embrace, both of them cling to each other as they cry.

"You are the best-behaved girl I know. I wish I could keep you forever, Mela. I love you so much it hurts." Fuck, I tug at the strands of my hair and make a split-second decision.

"Grab your shit." Allison snaps her gaze to me and the pain in her eye's morphs to hatred in a second.

"I need to pack her some things!" I narrow my eyes at her.

"Get your fucking purse, Allison. You both will be coming." Her eyes widen and she begins to shake her head. "Or, did you want to pack her things now and never see her again?" That has her clamping her mouth closed. Amelia turns back to me and her littles brow pull in together as she scowls up at me, sniffles and dabs her eyes with her sleeve.

"You rude man!" Allison snorts behind her and quickly tries to mask her reaction by coughing. I move toward them and don't miss how Allison shifts slightly so she is ready to pounce in front of Amelia if I try to harm her. It pisses me off but also makes me happy to know she would do anything to protect my daughter. I keep some space between her and me as I drop down to one knee. I just stare at her for a moment completely lost in her eyes. She looks so much like me—her hair color, her eyes, the way she scrunches her nose and lifts her lip when telling someone off.

"I'm sorry, I didn't mean to be rude to... Ally." I cut my gaze to Allison as I say that which causes her to roll her eyes. "How about I take you to get ice cream to say sorry properly and then we can go to my house for a swim?" I watch as Allison tenses out the corner of my eye but I ignore her. A bright smile stretches across my girl's face. She jumps up and down clapping before spinning to face Allison.

"Please, Ally, please please please." Allison pretends to think about it, knowing very fucking well she doesn't have a say in what happens.

"Only if you promise to keep your floaties on and let me put sunscreen on your face." She quirks a brow at my girl, who nods eagerly.

"I promise."

"Okay, go get your things while I speak to... King." Amelia scoffs and turns back to me with her brow furrowed.

"You name is King?" I nod. "That's cool." I can't stop my laugh that bubbles out of me. I never knew hearing a praise come from a kid could make you feel some type of way. As soon as she ducks into her room Allison is on her feet. I do the same and scowl down at her.

"What's your game here?" she whisper-shouts.

"I'll do whatever the fuck–"

"Shhh, you need to stop cussing in front of her!" she reprimands me like I'm a fucking kid and it pisses me off.

"I'll do whatever the fuck–" She strikes out and slaps her hand over my mouth with an angry look on her face. After a second, her eyes widen and she yanks her hand back like I burnt her. I can see the panic written all over her face.

"I... I didn't mean... it's just." She stops to take a deep breath, the sight of her all flustered is actually fucking funny. "Please don't cuss. It took me four weeks to get her to stop saying shit. I said it one time in front of her and everything was shit this, shit that, that's shit and I refuse to buy more bars of soap." I furrow my brow.

"Bars of soap?"

"Every time she said it she had to nibble on the bar of soap." Rage rises inside me. I strike out and clamp my hand around her neck, her eyes widen in fright as I get right in her face.

"You fucking made my daughter eat soap?" I whisper-shout.

"Let me go," she wheezes out.

"You ever do that shit again and I'll break your fucking neck." I release her with a shove and she stumbles back a couple steps rubbing her throat. Amelia chooses that moment to return. Allison quickly stands straight and drops her hand from around her throat and smiles at Amelia like nothing happened. How she fakes it stuns me. the woman is a class act, that's for fucking sure.

"I ready, Ally." It grates on my nerves that she looks to Allison for permission. I cut her off before she can answer.

"Allison just has to grab her things and then we can spend the afternoon swimming." Amelia squeals and jumps on the spot clapping her hands. Allison says nothing as she makes her way toward her room to grab whatever it is she needs. She should be on her knees fucking thanking for me letting her come and not taking Amelia from her now. The truth is the anguish in my daughter's tone is what gave me pause. Kiara had scolded me and told me that I couldn't just rip her away from the only parent she has known, but I ignored her. I'm Amelia's father and I should know what's best for her, not some washed-up collage drop out playing house with my kid.

The ride to my house is tense. Allison rides shotgun whilst Amelia is in back. I was fucking shocked when she walked out of her place with a child seat and argued with me right in front of Amelia that if I didn't put it in my car that Amelia would not be going. The bitch knew I wouldn't say or do anything to her in front of my kid. She'll pay for that stunt later.

"Wow, it's soooooo pretty." Her approval of my house has warmth filling inside me.

"Wait till you see the pool. It's wicked," I answer. Allison scoffs and mumbles under her breath. I glare at the side of her head. I park behind Bishop's car and hop out. With it being a Friday, I know Kiara and the twins are back for the weekend from school. I freeze as I open my door and pray that Bishop and she aren't fucking on the kitchen island like last weekend. That is a sight I wish I could bleach from my eyes, seeing my brothers naked ass isn't something I ever want to see again. I round the car to Amelia's side ready to grab her out, except fucking Allison beat me to it. She places Amelia on the ground beside her and when she meets my stare she just shrugs before looking down at my girl.

"Mela, why don't you go with King and I'll grab our bags." My heart soars when she nods eagerly. She rushes over and grips my hand in her tiny one, only managing to hold onto a finger.

"I ready." I smile down at her. I want nothing more than to reach down and pick her up so I can hold her close to me, but I also don't want to scare the shit out of her. As far as she is concerned, I'm some stranger her aunt has brought over and that's it. I walk toward the house and feel Allison hot on my heels. I wish she would have stayed fucking home but after how Amelia reacted earlier, I know that wasn't going to happen. I push the door and call out, no one answers and I don't hear any moaning so I'm fucking grateful. I lead them through the living room and straight out the back door to the pool. I find, Bishop, Kiara and the twins out here. The twins and Kiara are in the pool. Bishop stands on the side in his usual suit glaring down at his wife, he hates that her and the twins are close—she seems to be the only one Knight will let close to him since he got shot. He's kept all of us, including Rook, at arm's length. He's out for the season and doesn't even seem bothered he won't play for the football team. Their laughter all dies off as Bishop turns to me and clears his throat. The silences stretches as the four of them stare at the little girl at my side. I feel Amelia pull away and it guts me when I see her rush toward Allison, then hide behind her.

"Mela," Allison says and she bends down to her knees to face Mela with her back turned to my family, stupid woman. That is her first mistake. She should never turn her back on us, it could lead to her having a bullet in the back of her head. "Remember what we talked about?" Amelia nods but keeps her gaze on the ground. Rook swims to edge of the pool and climbs out, dripping water everywhere. He moves toward us and I pin him with a warning look. If he does anything to fuck this up for me, I'll beat his ass and make him regret the day he took his first breath. He ignores the look and moves to stand beside Allison. Both of them look up and Allison quickly jumps to her feet when she realizes it isn't me. I don't know why that fucking thought has me feeling slightly miffed.

"Now, who is this beautiful girl in the pretty pink swim suit?" Amelia looks up at Rook with stars in her eyes. It pisses me off that she smiles at him freely but is reserved with me. Rook turns to Allison and smiles. She returns it with a timid one of her own. "And who might this stunning masterpiece be?" I sneer at him but he ignores me.

"I'm Allison." She pulls Amelia into her side. "And this is Mela." Rook crouches down in front of his niece. I hold my breath waiting for him to announce himself as her uncle. I don't know if she would be able to handle knowing the truth yet, but she will in time.

"I'm Rook." Amelia looks up to Allison with a look on her face that I can't read. Allison nods her head encouragingly.

"Hi," my girl whispers shyly.

"Want to come for a swim?" Amelia nods enthusiastically. Rook reaches for her but Allison halts him with her words.

"She needs her floaties, just give me a minute." Rook nods and waits for Allison to dig through her bag and grab out these weird looking things that she slips on her arms. She nods to Rook, letting him know she is ready. My brother doesn't hesitate as he scoops her into his arms and takes off toward the pool. Panic swells inside me at the thought of him slipping with my daughter in his arms. At the sound of Allison's quiet laugh I cut my gaze to her and narrow my eyes as she shakes her head.

"What?" I snap.

"It sucks, doesn't it?"

"What does?"

"How easily worrying comes." I huff out a breath.

"Does it ever go away?" She shakes her head as she quietly says,

"No, it gets worse the older they get." Before I can have a go at her, Bishop helps Kiara from the pool and wraps a towel around her before they make their way toward us. I have no idea if Allison notices or not but she leans closer to me. Bishop and Kiara stop a few feet away. We stand here in awkward silence for a moment before Kiara rolls her eyes and steps forward with her hand extended toward Allison.

"I'm Kiara and this big brute is Bishop." Allison smiles warmly and shakes Kiara's hand.

"I'm Allison." Kiara rolls her eyes playfully as she steps back and snuggles into Bishop's side. A pang of envy shoots through me at the sight of them.

"We know," Kiara says, followed by a laugh. Allison furrows her brow at her.

"You do?" I grit my teeth in annoyance.

"We have heard a lot about you, girl. Now, why don't you come with me and I'll show you where to change while these guys talk about our asses as we walk away?" Allison chokes on air and her eyes widen as she shakes her head.

"I didn't bring a suit." Kiara shrugs, grips Allison's hand and starts to lead her away.

"You can borrow one of mine." Allison yanks Kiara to a halt and turns back to me.

"Can you... can you please... watch her?" I glare down

at her ready to tell her where to go before Bishop cuts me off.

"You have my word, she will be safe." Bishop's words seem to put her at ease. She smiles her thanks him and nods before following Kiara toward the pool house.

Chapter Five

Allison

I feel so awkward and all types of wrong borrowing her bathing suit. The bottoms are a bikini cut so the bottom of my ass cheeks hang out. The top is small and my breasts don't exactly fit it properly but I don't have to worry as I've been in here for at least ten minutes and Amelia is out there with them. I come out of the bathroom and find Kiara in the living room. Her eyes widen at the sight of me and I begin to feel self-conscious.

"Damn, girl, how do you get all of that?" I can't help the laughter that bubbles out of me. "I hate that you look better in my own bikini than I do." I scoff, has this girl seen a mirror? She is fucking gorgeous. Long black hair and pale as fuck blue eyes, she has the perfect body to boot.

"Please, I haven't worn a bathing suit since..." I cut

myself off and drop my gaze. Kiara rushes over and grips one of my hands in hers.

"Don't do that." I slowly lift my gaze to hers in question.

"Do what?" She blows out a breath before answering.

"I love each of these boys but let me help a sister out." I nod eagerly. "Do not give into them. You stand your ground and fight for what you want. If you don't, they will walk all over you." I eye her and shake my head.

"They have the money to take her from me. I'm not like you all, I don't have a trust fund–" Kiara laughs and it grates on my nerves. I yank my hand free and glare at her. "Just because I don't have money doesn't mean you're better than me." Her eyes harden as she stares at me and I ready myself for the onslaught.

"What the fuck makes you think I'm rich? I'm a scholarship kid. I used to fight every Friday night at the shack in down town to make money just to survive. I may be with Bishop but that doesn't mean I have money. Don't judge a fucking book by its cover, Allison. We all aren't what we seem." Shame washes over me.

"I'm so sorry, I should never have said what I did. I'm just..." I take a deep breath and tell her the truth. "I'm so fucking scared he will take her from me. I'm all that girl has known since the moment she was born. I can't afford a lawyer and even if I could, I don't have a leg to stand on. He's her father and I'm just her... Ally." Kiara shocks the shit out of me when she wraps her arms around me and pulls me to her, hugging me. I didn't know how much I needed this until now. Before I can let my emotions get the better of me she pulls back and smiles at me cockily.

"Listen here, we are going to go out there and you are going to hold your head high. Don't let King see he is getting to you, fight back. Just for the record, I voted against King taking her from you. I knew it wouldn't be a good idea to rip a kid away from the only mother she has ever known." Her words send a warmth through me, I give myself a mental pep talk before taking a deep breath and standing tall, nodding my head for Kiara to lead the way. As soon as we round the corner from the pool house, I feel their gazes on me I choose to focus on Mela who is now sitting atop a huge unicorn float.

"Look me Ally, I got big one." I give her a double thumbs up and smile wide, she looks so happy. Rook and the other guy who I know to be his twin Knight, are standing on either side of her making sure she doesn't fall in. I know who each of these guys are but only from the tabloids. I follow Kiara over to the loungers where King and Bishop sit. She takes the spot between his legs and rests back against his chest. He looks down at her like she is the very oxygen he needs to breathe. I sneak a glance at King to find his gaze already on me. When I see anger in his green eyes it stumps me.

"What the fuck are you wearing?" he snaps. I turn toward Mela and sigh in relief that she didn't just hear him berating me.

"Can you keep your voice down please, she doesn't need to hear you speaking to me like that and it's a bathing suit." Kiara shoots me a look telling me to not give in. I close my eyes for a second and ready myself for the battle I'm sure is going to follow. I don't wait for his reply as I turn on my heel, run torward the pool and jump, making a huge splash. I smile to myself as I break the surface, Mela claps her hands and cheers for me. Rook and Knight are both laughing. I follow their gazes and spin around in the water to see King standing there clothed, dripping wet and glaring at me. I smile up at him innocently and wave before swimming over to Mela and the twins.

Kiara wouldn't relent until I agreed that Mela and I would stay for dinner. Mela is absolutely taken by the twins. The three of them are all crowded at the coffee table in the living room playing mouse trap. A pang hits me in the chest at the sight. She has been missing out on all of this because of me.

"I haven't seen my brother smile in months." I startle at the sound of his voice. I turn to the side and stare up at Bishop as he takes a sip of whiskey from his tumbler.

"Why not?" He doesn't look at me when he answers.

"He went through some shit. Today is the first time I haven't seen the ghosts of his past pulling him under because of Mela." It warms my heart to know Mela's beautiful soul can bring light into one of her uncle's lives. My warmth evaporates when he speaks again. "You so much as think of keeping that child from her father or hurting him the same way your sister did, you won't live to see your twenty-second birthday." I gape up at him in horror. He lazily swings his gaze to me and I can see it in the depths of his brown eyes, he isn't joking. I gulp loudly and nod. I was stupid to think Mela was missing out. I know now I did the right thing by shielding her away from her father's side of the family. They are killers and this isn't a world for a child to be raised in. I steel myself and hold Bishop's gaze as I answer low enough for only him to hear.

"I know you have all dug up information about me and may think you know who I am but you don't." The look in his eyes has me quaking but I won't back down. "I'll never give her up without a fight. I raised her. I was the one to love her first and I know who you and your family are." He raises his brows but I'm not done yet. "I don't care. Mela is everything to me and I will not allow you or your brother to take her from me. She's my..." I cut myself off before I can finish and drop my gaze.

"She's your what?" I spin around so fast I nearly slip. Bishop grips my arm to steady me and I don't miss the way King's gaze drops to my arm that Bishop holds.

"Huh?" I splutter as Bishop releases his hold on me. I spy Kiara out of the corner of my eye stalking toward us.

"She's. Your. What?" He makes sure to enunciate each word like he is speaking to a toddler. He moves so close that his chest brushes against me and I have to crane my neck back to look up at him. "Answer me, Allison!" How can a man look so strikingly beautiful and yet be a demonic monster inside. King's boyishly good looks lull you into thinking he's a good guy, when he's not.

"She's my... girl," I mutter, he narrows his eyes at me.

"Nah, that's not what you were going to–"

"Hey, Ally." I turn to the side to see Rook waving me over. I don't even hesitate, I move toward them but King wraps an arm around my waist hauling me back against his rock-hard chest. I gasp. Mela looks to me in confusion, so I quickly wipe the surprised look from my face and smile happily at her.

"I'm just gonna be a minute then I'll join you. Okay, Meelz." She begrudgingly nods clearly not sold on my excuse. King doesn't utter a tord as he lifts me from the ground and walks us into the kitchen. Bishop and Kiara both stare at us. He looks pissed but Kiara fights the smile trying to break free. He keeps going until we reach a games room before he finally releases his hold on me. My relief is short lived when a hand wraps around my neck and I'm slammed back against the wall. I stare up at him in horror, certain he is going to kill me where I stand while Mela is in the other room.

"She isn't yours. You're not her fucking mother! She is my daughter and you are only here until she gets comfortable enough to be around me. Do I make myself clear?" Tears burn the backs of my eyes as I nod. He isn't done though, as he leans down until we are eye to eye. "You so much as think of pulling even half the shit your sister did–" I cut him off, so tired of the threats on my life.

"Kill me then!" I taunt him. "I don't care anymore. If you take her from me then death will be better than living in a world where I can't be around her." For a second, one split second I see remorse in his eyes before he quickly masks it.

"You don't know half of it, Allison. Your sister wasn't the angel you think she was. You will spend the night here with Amelia–"

"I have work!" I interject. He scoffs and rolls his eyes.

"You'll make your shift at that piece of shit diner where you make ends meet." I flinch. I hate that he can look down his nose at me, not knowing what I have been through.

Chapter Six

King

Bishop and I sit in his office drinking a glass of whiskey each. Amelia is upstairs having a bath with Allison. I had Luka go into town and get them both some clothes for the night and whatever other fucking shit girls need. The twins have gone off to do whatever the fuck it is they do and Kiara is studying for exams.

"We need to make a move soon. The Romello's are preparing to rise against us and I can't have that type of unease." I sigh and run a hand through my hair, I wish I could just focus on getting to know my daughter, but unfortunately we are at war and if I want to make this city safe for her, then I need to help take down the other families.

"What about this shit with the Russian's?"

"We need the manpower before we can go after them,

taking down the other three families will give us that. Until that happens, we have no choice but to be vigilant and watch our fucking backs." I nod my agreement.

"When do you want to strike?" At the sound of her laughter, I automatically turn my head toward the open door to see my little girl standing there in her fuzzy pink pajamas and unicorn slippers. She has a huge smile on her face as she rushes toward me.

"Mela, no!" I hear Allison shout as my girl runs to me and jumps onto my lap. I still for a moment and cut a glance to the doorway where a terrified Allison stands. Mela wraps her arms around my neck hugging me. As if I've done this a million times, my arms automatically wrap around her and everything shifts inside me. "I'm so sorry, she just took off to find you and—"

"She's fine, she can go wherever she likes in this house." Bishop's words are firm but not aggressive, I look up to Allison as she stands beside me twisting her hands in front of her. My eyes take on a mind of their own as they drink in what she is wearing. I know I told Luka to buy her ugly shit but fuck me, she makes the cheap shit look sexy as hell. Her hair is wet and still dripping. She has a plain black crop top thing on that exposes her toned stomach and the sleep shorts are so fucking tiny if she bent over her ass would be out. I'm going to fucking kill Luka for this, the bastard!

"Thank you sooooo much." Amelia pulls back and smiles so wide it must hurt her face. I stare at her confused before Allison cuts in and explains.

"I told her you got her the pajamas and slippers." I look back at my little girl and smile. A pair of clothes and she is acting like I bought her a fucking car. I hate that the credit for her gratefulness goes to Allison and the way she has raised her. "Is there any way we could, maybe if it's okay, please go back home?" I glare up at Allison in warning, her expression changes from timid to worried. "I need Mr. Snaggles, she won't sleep without him and I didn't bring him with us today. I'm sorry." I feel like a dick when she drops her gaze to her feet and stands there awkwardly. I look to Amelia who now seems upset by my reaction to Allison.

"Hey Mela?" She turns to Bishop and smiles shyly. "What if Kiara and I take you to pick up your toy—" Amelia gasps and cuts him off. Allison rolls her eyes and stares up at the celling as if this has happened before.

"Meelz..." Allison tries to warn but she ignores her.

"He is not a toy! He is real and needs loving all the days and nights." Bishop looks to me as if expecting me to know what the fuck that means. We both swing our gazes to Allison who looks slightly embarrassed.

"She... she..." She stops and looks to Mela. "Would you like to explain who he is?" She nods eagerly.

"He's part of my daddy." My eyes widen and I reel back in shock. Allison drops down into the chair beside me and keeps her gaze focused on her lap.

"How so?" Bishop asks. Thank fuck he's recovered quicker than me.

"Daddy had to go away and make bad men better so he left me Mr. Snaggles." I stare at her dumfounded, unsure of what the fuck I say to that. I can feel Bishop gawking at me but I still can't form any words.

"How about you and I go find Kiara and we pick up Mr. Snaggles and get some ice cream... as long as that is okay with... Allison?"

"She needs her seat from King's car," Allison whispers. Bishop stands and comes around to grab Amelia from my lap. Allison climbs to her feet but Bishop's words stop her.

"I'll take King's car. Don't act surprised when I tell you we have a key to your apartment. I also have four younger siblings, I know what I'm doing, Allison and if I don't, let's hope to hell Kiara does."

"Um, okay but if she needs me—?"

"I have your number and by the end of tonight you will have all of ours as well." I peer over my shoulder and watch as Bishop leaves. Amelia is smiling in his hold waving to Allison. I look at her and I can see the worry lines dotting her features, for the first time since trailing her a couple weeks ago I feel something other than deep hatred, a sense of appreciation flows through me. She may have kept my kid from me but she still kept the notion of her father alive in her life. I stand from my chair and Allison slowly turns to face me with her hands clasped in front of her, she's looking everywhere but at me.

"Why did you do it?" Her whole-body tenses, she slowly lifts her blue eyes to me and I can't get a read on what she is thinking and it pisses me off.

"S-she already lost her mom and I just... I couldn't stomach the thought of her losing her father as well and I..." She blows out a whoosh of air and drops her gaze to floor, I'm not having it. I close the space between us and grip her chin between my fingers and lift her face until we lock eyes.

"Don't look down. I want your eyes on me every time you speak." Her mouth opens in shock but she nods regardless. "Now, explain to me why you had her think I left a soft toy for her instead of being present."

"I couldn't give her... you, so I gave her something else that would ease the pain of you not being present. I know you have every right to be mad at me..." I scoff and drop my hold on her face as I step and shake my head.

"Mad? You think I'm fucking mad? You have no fucking

idea how I feel. Don't you dare stand there and act like you know how I feel." She nibbles her bottom lip and nods.

"You're right, I don't know how you feel." Before my eyes I watch her regret turn to anger and it sparks something inside me to see her ready to challenge me. "You know what, fuck you. I never asked for any of this. I did what I could for her. As soon as she was born I was there. Christine died three weeks later, what the fuck was I supposed to do? Was I supposed to come here and knock on the mafia's door and say 'hey, King, you don't know me but here's your daughter?'" She's yelling now, I don't interrupt, I want to hear everything she has to say. "You would have laughed in my face. I know you and Christine never got on. You were both bad for each other but that little baby didn't need to pay for yours and her mistakes. I'm sorry you feel shafted but if I was faced with the same choice again, I wouldn't do anything differently. She is fucking perfect, she is so smart and kind. I gave up everything to raise her, King, so don't you dare stand there and judge me for my choices." I can't stand to hear more of this. I grab her face between my hands and smash my lips against hers, effectively silencing her. She struggles in my hold for a second before her shock bleeds from her body and she gets lost in the kiss. Just as I deepen it, she yanks free and stumbles back a step, her eyes wide with fright at what just happened. She reaches up tentatively and touches her lips whilst staring at me. I don't want to think too much on what I just fucking did, so I turn and storm from the room. I make it up the stairs and just about get to my room before Knight's door swings open. He stands there staring at me for a moment. I'm just about to carry on to my room but his words hold me in place.

"She isn't like her sister. Don't hurt her, King." I stare at him for a second taken back by his remark. Knight never showed any care toward Christine.

"How would you know?" My little brother steps out of his room and moves close so that we are nearly chest to chest.

"I just do. Don't do anything to hurt her. Amelia needs her."

"Don't fucking tell me what my daughter needs!"

"Pull your fucking head out of your ass and realize that Allison is what she needs!"

———

I check my watch for the dozenth time waiting for Bishop to fucking get back with Amelia. Allison sits on the couch next to Rook, waiting as well. It's nearly eight at night and she should be here... with *us*. What the fuck? Since when did I think of Allison and me as an *us*? The sound of the door opening has me snapping out of my thoughts and sighing in relief at the sight of Bishop and Kiara walking in with Amelia cuddled into her uncle's chest. Allison jumps to her feet and runs over to them grabbing Amelia, who is half asleep, from Bishop, holding her brown teddy.

"You could have called. It's late and she should have been in bed nearly an hour ago!" Bishop stares down at Allison as if she has lost her fucking mind for daring to speak to him like that. Me? Hearing her berate my brother, the mafia Don, has my cock getting hard and it shouldn't! I want to torment her and wreak havoc on her life for hiding my kid from me. Kiara steps forward and rests her hand on Allison's forearm.

"I'm sorry we were so late, there was a... complication." Allison clutches Amelia tighter to her chest. I make my way over and stand beside her, resting a hand on my daughter's back.

"What type of complication?" I growl. Before Bishop can answer my question Kiara pipes up.

"Ally, why I don't show you and Mela to your room?" Allison shakes her head.

"No, I want to know if she is in danger!" I can hear the hysteria in her voice and know I need to stop it before it disturbs my girl. I turn and grab Allison's face between my hands, her frightened gaze locks on to mine.

"I'll handle it. No harm will come to Amelia." She nods and it shocks the shit out of me that she trusts me at my word to keep her safe. She follows after Kiara and I stand here watching them walk up the stairs. "And you," I mutter below my breath. I know Bishop heard but he doesn't say a thing, instead he calls for Rook to get Knight and meet us in the office.

I pace the length of Bishop's office. "What the fuck do you mean followed?" I snap at my brother.

"When we got to her place there was a car parked there. I circled the block twice and when they made me, they took off." Fuck! I ram my hand through my hair and feel my temper rise. No, it's not just anger it's... fear. I've never had a weakness before, except for my brothers and sister, but now, I have a weakness that isn't big enough to defend herself. I look to the others and see both Knight and Rook looking livid. Mav and Luka lean against the wall with murderous looks on their faces. I know my family will go to war for my girl.

"We take them out. The Ramello family has been

hedging for our spot since we took out the Ramano's, we need to strike now!" The conviction in Rook's voice is awe inspiring. Just one afternoon with Amelia and already he is protective as shit over her.

"They can't go back." Knight's quietly spoken words have me studying him. Something is going on with him and from the way he looks to Bishop, I know he is in on whatever it is.

"If they don't, then they will know we are onto them. We need to find a way in with the Russian's and exploit their weakness. We know the other families are working with them so if we keep this up, we will find their source." I glare at Bishop.

"You're willing to use my kid as fucking bait?" He stands from his chair and rests his hands on the edge of his desk as he leans over to stare at me.

"I would never risk the safety of my niece, don't even question me on that again! Allison needs to return to her apartment but Mela, she will remain here with us where she is safe." He's saying everything that I want but why does it feel fucking wrong to do this? I want her with me always so she can get to know me and my family but I know that her being without Allison will destroy her.

"She can't stay there unprotected!" Knight steals the words from my mouth.

"She won't be. Gage can stay with her and keep—" I sneer and cut Bishop off.

"No. Gage will stay the fuck away from her. I'll be with Allison and Amelia." Bishop tries to cut me off but I push on. "They want to exploit my weakness? Let those cunts try because if they make a move, it'll be with me there not that fucker Gage!"

Chapter Seven

Allison

The ride to work is filled with tension and I hate it. I keep turning back to check on Mela who is completely unaware of the danger we are in. King told me about what had happened and I disclosed that I have felt like I have been followed for a while now. The look in his eyes had me scared shitless. He said it wasn't him following that close. I was shocked to learn he had been following me for a while. He said Mela and I could return to our home under the condition that he would be staying with us. I wanted to rebuke him but how could I do that? My pride doesn't mean anything when it comes to keeping Mela safe.

"What does she do when you work weekends?" I startle at his softly spoken question, I turn and look at him, he wears a plain black shirt and jeans. He doesn't dress like

Bishop or the twins, he dresses for comfort not style. What he doesn't understand is with the way he dresses and rocking converses like that he gives off Paul Walker vibes and it works for him. I shake my head to clear those thoughts from my mind, he's my niece's father and is in the fucking mob!

"She comes with me. I can't get a sitter so I have to take her with me." He nods but I can see the cogs in his mind turning with an unasked question. "Just say whatever it is you want to say."

"How long is your shift?" His question throws me a bit.

"I only work the morning on the weekends because of Mela."

"What if, instead of her waiting for you, I... took her shopping?" Fear sparks to life inside me. I gulp and begin to squirm in my chair. "I... I'll bring her back," he grits out through clenched teeth as we pull up to the curb outside the diner I work at. I turn back to face Mela and when she beams at me I melt.

"Meelz?"

"Yes?"

"W-would you like to spend the day with King?" Her little brows furrow as she looks between me and King, who is now looking at her as well with a warm smile on his face.

"Will you come?" I shake my head as I reach back and brush my knuckles over her cheek.

"I can't, baby girl. I have to work." A cunning look enters her eyes.

"So, I can get my tea party set?" I chuckle and nod.

"Yeah, baby, a couple more shifts, then we can go get it."

"Okay, I go with King." I spy him out of the corner of my eye and flinch when she calls him by his name. I smile and bid her goodbye, then ask King if I can have a word outside with him. I move to the curb and wait for him to join me. He shoves his hands in his pockets and I stand here awkward as fuck, not sure how to start this conversation.

"What's up?" he prompts. I release a whoosh of air before I meet his gaze.

"I-I know this is a fucked-up situation but I just wanted to thank you for yesterday and not announcing who... you are to her." He nods but I can see in his eyes he has something to say.

"I want her to know, Allison, soon. I'm not her friend. I'm her father and she has a right to know." I steel my spine and clench my hands into fists at my sides.

"Are you gonna take off and leave her? Will you be present for school days? What about when she's sick and cries all day, can you hack that? Because if you can't—" He cuts me off when he strikes out, grips my face and slams his lips against mine. Like fucking putty I melt into him. He shouldn't have this effect on me, I don't even know him and for fuck's sake, he is my dead sister's ex and the father to Amelia! I push against his chest and he pulls back with a cocky grin on his face. I want to smack the look right off.

"Now that shut you up." I glower at him while he just chuckles. "We can talk about this shit tonight, okay?"

"Okay," I mutter as I storm past him but he calls out making me pause.

"Luka will be here with you today. You won't see him but he will be around." My eyes widen in surprise. "Don't look so shocked, cherry pie, you're important to Mela so that makes you important to me." I hate that my heart skips a beat hearing him say that. I nod like a dick and quickly head into work.

My shift has dragged on and Kevin has been a royal pain in my ass all day. Apparently Sally said he saw me kissing King. I don't know how me kissing King would cause him to be a dick when I have made it clear I have no interest in him. I've passed him twice today to head into the kitchen and the sick prick has grabbed my ass. If I didn't need this job so badly, I would knee him in the fucking balls and walk out!

"Allison!" his voice booms across the busy diner and has me cringing. I smile to the couple whose order I just took and quickly scurry behind the counter to meet him.

"What's wrong?" He narrows his beady eyes at me. His breath huffs out and fans across my face causing me to have to fight the gag from the stench of cigarettes.

"Want to tell me why you have a guy in your section who hasn't placed a single order?" I furrow my brow and follow his gaze to a man who is dressed impeccably in a suit and sticks out, I shake my head.

"I didn't see him, I'll go now." As I turn to walk over to the man Kevin slaps my ass and I have to grit my teeth or risk screaming at him. As I head toward the man, I find his disapproving stare on Kev. I hate that most people here just saw what he did. I know I'm red from shame by the time I reach his table. I pull out my pad and pen and say,

"What can I get you, sir?" I keep my gaze down, something about this guy has me feeling on edge.

"You can take a seat?" I slowly lift my gaze to his and find his piercing stare looking right at me.

"Why?" A slow smirk graces his handsome face.

"Because, shit is about to go down and I think you should have a front seat to the drama." Before I can answer him the front door to the diner slams open and bangs so loudly it draws everyone's attention. I gape at the sight of

King, Knight and some other guy storming in here with angry looks on their faces. I follow King's line of sight to Kevin and my mouth drops open.

"Hey, you break that door—" Kevin doesn't get a chance to finish what he is saying before King grips the front of his shirt and punches him in the face. I scream and try to dart forward but the man grips my arm. I turn back to him and try to yank free.

"He's going to get arrested," I shout at the man.

"Nah, he's King Murdoch. The cops would never touch him and plus, that fat fucker had it coming from how he has been treating you." That's when it all clicks into place.

"You're Luka?" He smiles wide and nods. The sound of King's voice draws my attention back to them, customers are rushing out of the diner at the sight of Kevin getting the shit beaten out of him.

"You ever fucking touch her like that again and I'll put a fucking bullet between your eyes, you cunt!" Kevin's face is covered in blood and he splutters causing blood to spray on King.

"I didn't touch—" King punches him again causing Kev to scream out.

"You fat cunt, you're done in this town." King releases him with a hard shove. Kev stumbles back and trips causing him to fall on his ass. Sally stands off to the side in shock. I wish I could say I feel bad but Kevin deserved what he just got. He has been doing it to Sally for years and a couple other girls as well. King turns to Sally and she tenses in fear. He digs into his pocket and I freeze thinking he is going to pull a gun, instead he pulls out a wad of cash and holds it out to her. She gingerly reaches out and takes it. "You'll be compensated more by the end of the day. I'll have enough wired to your account for you to retire... Now leave." Sally looks to me but King shifts so he blocks her view. "She's with me, now go." I expect her to leave like everyone else in my life.

"I'm gonna need to hear that from her." I look around and find the diner is now empty except for us. King nods and steps aside so Sally can see me. Luka lets me go and I move toward her but King snaps out his arm and hauls me into his side. She looks from me to him clearly trying to see if I'm in danger, so I smile reassuringly.

"Take the money, Sal, go back to Georgia and enjoy those grandbabies."

"You gonna be okay, girl? Where is Miss Mela?" Her concern for Mela has my heart bursting inside me.

"I'm okay... I think Mela is—"

"With family," King cuts in. I pull out of his hold and wrap Sally in a hug, getting choked up a bit. She has been like a mother and grandmother to both Mela and I for the past couple years. I don't know if I would have made it here without her.

"Thank you, Sally, for loving me and Mela. We wouldn't be where we are without you." I pull back and smile at her and wipe the tears that fall from her eyes. "Now, you take this rich schmucks money and go live your best life. I promise Mela and I will be fine."

"You don't got a job now, girl." Before I answer, King cuts in.

"She doesn't need one. I got her and Mela." Sally hugs me again before leaving the diner. King takes my hand and leads me to the idling Range Rover at the curb. Knight hops in the back whilst Luka and the other guy cross the road to an Escalade. King opens the passenger door for me and I slip in. I turn in my seat and find Rook and Mela in the back, she's fast asleep with Mr. Snaggles snuggled into her side.

"Causing drama already, aye?" I look to Rook and flinch at the gleeful look in his eyes. King jumps in beside me and takes off.

"I didn't mean to," I whisper.

"You didn't do shit. That cunt got what was coming to him." The protectiveness in Knight's tone has me staring at him in wonder. I can see from the look in his brown eyes that this boy has demons he is fighting inside and for some reason I feel like I have a kindred spirit in him.

Chapter Eight

King

As soon as she walks into her apartment she freezes. I move past her and head to Mela's room to put her in her new carriage style bed. I place a kiss on her forehead before going back out to join the twins and Allison, who's gazing around in shock. Rook makes himself at home by dropping down onto the new sofa and kicking his feet up on the small table in front. Knight drops down next to him and pulls out his phone. Allison turns to me.

"What happened?" I flick my head motioning for her to follow me, she does. Once we enter her tiny bedroom she gasps, and looks around at all her new furniture. She turns to me with wide eyes. "I can't afford all of this," she screeches.

"I never fucking asked you to!" She reels back in fear at

the cold tone of my voice. "It's a gift, Allison, for you and Mela."

"I'm not fucking you!" Now, my eyes widen as I throw my head back and laugh. It takes me a second to get myself under control before I meet her heated glare again. "I'm serious, just because you brought all this fancy stuff—"

"Want me to kiss you again?" She stumbles back a step and shakes her head but I can see the lust in her blue eyes. "Good, then shut up. I have some shit to handle with Bishop then I'll be back. The twins will stay with you and Mela. Tonight, we'll sit down and talk shit out. Allison, I want answers." She takes a deep breath and nods.

Bishop and I are looking over the blueprints of the Ramello's compound with Luka, Mav, Gage and Kiara. That bloody girl has a thirst for blood just like Bishop, they really are the perfect pair. As we ready ourselves to head out and scope out the compound, Bishop calls me back. I close the office door behind myself and wait for him to say whatever it is he has to say.

"I need the truth."

"Of what?" He slips his mask into place and I know now that my brother is gone, he has been replaced by the leader of the family.

"Who told you about Christine and Amelia?"

"It was an anonymous letter. It had no name. Just a copy of her birth certificate, which I'm not listed on, and a photo of her and Allison at Christine's grave." Bishop eyes me for a moment before speaking.

"How did you know she was yours then?" I scoff.

"She looks exactly like me, Bish. Allison confirmed it

when I confronted her and that was all I needed." He opens his mouth but I cut him off. "You ask me to get a DNA test and I'll punch you in the fucking mouth. She's mine, Bishop." He nods solemnly.

"King, you need to talk to Knight." I tense at the mention of our little bother.

"Why? Shouldn't you be more focused on finding Car?" He growls.

"I know where she is. She has a tail on her all hours of the day and night. Don't fucking question my loyalty to my family, I'd never let her get too far." I nod, of course the control freak wouldn't. I don't blame Car for leaving. This family can suck the life out of you and she has been through so fucking much already. That's the only reason Bish and I haven't gone after her because unlike Kiara, Car isn't a fighter, she's a runner. "Speak to Knight."

"Why?" A shudder rolls through Bishop and that has me on edge. Bishop never reacts to anything except if it involves Kiara.

"I would take the blame for the rest of my life if it meant he didn't have to have you look at him the way you look at me."

"The fuck are you talking about, Bishop?" I'm about to lose my shit soon. He moves toward me and places a hand on my shoulder. I want to knock it away but I remain still. We haven't seen eye to eye for a long fucking time since he told me to give up Christine and she died months later.

"It wasn't me, brother," he whispers.

"Huh?" Dread begins to pool inside me.

"I took the blame because it was easier for you to think it was me—"

"Spit it the fuck out, now!" I snap. He nods but I can see he is hesitant.

"Okay, fine. Here it is, brother. I told you to get rid of her because she was fucking Knight. She used you to get to our brother and asked him to do something—" I stumble back and smack against the wall shaking my head, denying what he is saying. We were toxic but she wouldn't do that to me, would she? "I never killed her, King. I swear to you on my honor. It wasn't me, brother. You need to talk to Knight."

"What the fuck for?" I yell.

"Because there is more to the story and it is his to tell, not mine."

After scoping out the joint for a few hours, I drop Luka and Mav back to their cars and head back to Allison's. I need to hear what Knight has to say, Bishop wouldn't throw him under the bus or rat him out like that if it wasn't important. The further I have pulled away from Bish, Knight has done the same to me and I can feel it in my bones that Bishop is telling the truth. I scan the street as I park and I see a few cars but they don't look out of the ordinary. I race up the stairs and use my key to open the door. It's nearly midnight so I know Amelia won't be up and it guts me, but in order to keep her safe, I need to take down these families in order for her to be free of the burden we were all faced with. Knight and Rook jump to their feet at the sound of the door opening, Knight has his gun in hand and I quirk a brow at him as he tucks in back into his shorts.

"How'd it go?" I ignore Rook's question as I grab a beer from the fridge and drop down into the recliner opposite them.

"Allison asleep?" I ask instead of answering.

"Yeah, she tried to wait up for you but I think the excitement of today wore her out." He chuckles but Knight and I remain silent. I slowly look to Knight. He won't even meet my gaze and I haven't the time or patience to baby him, so I cut right to the chase.

"What happened with you and Christine?" He doesn't flinch or even react, Rook on the other hand gapes at his twin.

"The fuck are you talking about, Knight—" Knight cuts Rook off.

"It was all going good, she was going to tell you the truth about us, but then something changed." My hand clenches my beer so tight I fear I may shatter it. He's speaking like a robot with no emotion. "She pulled back from me. I tried to get the information out of her but she wouldn't say. You two broke up and she was... Then months passed and she called..." I can see in his eyes he is reliving the memory. Hearing my brother speak about the woman I loved and how he was fucking her behind my back kills me. I want to beat the shit out of him and hurt him till he bleeds, but I guess I think I always knew Knight fancied Christine.

"What the fuck did she ask you, Knight?" Rook hedges his twin. Knight finally looks me in the eyes and I see it in the depths of his brown eyes just how broken my brother is over this.

"She called me, she told me we could be together and that we needed to meet. I showed up and was ready to come to you that night and tell you the truth, that we loved each other but then she got out of the car. Her belly was so big... I choked up. I thought it was mine and that's why she called." I stare at him in horror. He knew about Amelia and never said a word! "She told me we could be together if I did one tiny thing for her..."

"What was it?" I ask him barely above a whisper. I'm sure I know what he is about to say and I prepare myself for it.

"She said I had to kill you." Rook gasps in horror, while I just stare at Knight. I figured the crazy bitch would do something like that.

"What happened after that?" I push, his eyes glaze over as he recites what happened.

"She told me the baby wasn't mine. I asked if it was yours and she said no. My heart broke. She told me we could say it was mine if I just did her the tiny favor of ending your life. She wanted me to kill my own fucking brother!" he shouts, then scrubs a hand down his face. Rook moves forward and places a hand on his back in comfort, but I can't. I need to know what he decided.

"What happened next?" I can hear the rage in my own voice. He looks to me and I see it in his eyes, the truth.

"I told her she had lost her fucking mind. She fucked with my head so bad, King. I thought I loved her." I nod.

"She's good at that," I admit.

"I couldn't do it. I don't remember what happened after that but she took off and I chased after her. I thought she was going to go after you so I followed but it was raining and she was speeding..." He stops speaking as a sob breaks free. I wait for him to continue but he's crying so hard.

"She lost control of her car and spun out." I turn to see Allison standing near the kitchen. I want to jump to my feet but I can't move. "She crashed into a tree, was rushed to hospital and they tried to save her but they couldn't. There was a choice to be made and I... made it." Tears stream down her cheeks.

"What choice?" Rook asks. Knight has his face buried

into Rook's chest as he cries, the sight breaks me. Allison keeps her tearful gaze on me as she answers.

"I love that girl more than you will ever understand because I chose her. I chose to save Amelia over her mother." My eyes widen and my mouth drops open in shock. "I knew from the start you were her father. Christine knew she could manipulate Knight, she wanted one of you to make her a kept woman so she could live the lavish lifestyle of a *mafia* wife." She spits the word like it burns her tongue. "You wouldn't commit to her, so she went after Knight. I don't know why she didn't come to you about the baby, she never wanted her. I begged Christine not to get rid of the baby. She tried." Anger like I have never felt before surges inside me. "She was too far along. She was my sister, but she wasn't a saint."

"What did you do, Allison?" I say barely above a whisper, she wipes the tears from her eyes and stands tall as she moves toward me leaving a couple feet of space between us as she holds my stare.

"I told them to save the baby. They tried to help Christine but she died three weeks later in the hospital. I lied, she never filled out the birth certificate, I did. I never named you on it because I blamed you and your family for taking my sister from me." I strike out and wrap my hand around her throat and squeeze, the twins jump to their feet and try to pry me off her but they can't.

"You fucking hid her from me!" I scream in her face, she doesn't crumble under my wrath.

"I did! And I would fucking do it again if it meant keeping her out of your sick twisted world." I release her with a shove and watch as she falls to her ass.

"Your sister was a cunt!" I scream down at her. "So are you!" I storm past her and grab Amelia from her bed, making sure to grab the fucking teddy. Allison jumps to her feet and tries to come for Mela but I shove her back she stumbles into Knight who grips her to keep her steady. I look at both of them in disgust. Mela stirs in my hold but I don't even look at her as I focus on these traitors.

"Please, punish me but don't take her!" Allison screams, tears pouring from her eyes.

"You and my brother deserve each other. I'll be back for her things tomorrow. You so much as try and come for her, I'll have you arrested for kidnapping." I turn and head for the door ignoring Rook's angry glare. Mela begins to squirm in my hold and cries for Allison, who is screaming for her.

"Ally!" Mela cries out but I ignore her as I leave.

Chapter Nine

King

Mela hasn't stopped crying and calling out for Allison. Kiara is trying to calm her but nothing is working. Bishop and I stand outside my room. Amelia cries harder for Allison whenever she sees me, so I thought it best to leave Kiara with her. It fucking kills me that I can't be the one to comfort my girl. I should be able to ease her fears and pain but all she fucking wants is Allison!

"What happened?" I don't look at Bishop as I answer.

"Knight told me what happened."

"And then what?" He knows me well enough to know that something big would have happened for me to take Mela from Allison.

"She came out and told me that she knew I was the

father from the start and didn't name me on the birth certificate so she could keep Mela. Christine wanted to get rid of the baby and Allison stopped her! She wanted to kill my fucking daughter, Bishop!" I shout as I tug at the strands of my hair. He reaches out and places a hand on my shoulder about to say something when the room door flings open.

"Guys, something's wrong." I push past Kiara and freeze when I see my girl struggling to breath.

"What the fuck happened?" I shout.

"I don't know!" Kiara answers in a panic.

"What do we do?" I ask.

"Fuck!" Bishop snaps before pulling his phone from his pocket and dialing someone, I rush over to Mela and gather in my arms and hate that I don't know what to do. "Where are you, she needs you?" I stare at Bishop for a moment and it clicks, Allison. "Upstairs, King's room hurry she can't breathe." Bishop hangs up his phone as I try and soothe my girl and rock her in my arms, I hear the front door smash open then footsteps pounding against the wooden floors. Bishop and Kiara step out of the way as Allison and the twins come running in. She doesn't hesitate to jump straight on the bed and yank Mela from my arms, cradling her against her chest as rummages through her purse for something.

"It's okay, baby girl. Hang on, okay? Deep breaths, baby. You know how to do this." Mela nods up at Allison whilst gasping for air and it fucking kills me to see it.

"Do something!" I scream at her. She cuts me a scathing look.

"Shut the fuck up, asshole. She's having an asthma attack because of you!" she screams right in my face. She places a white mask thing over Mela's face and gets her to hold it while she places an inhaler in the other end and pumps it twice, the mask fills with what looks like smoke before Mela inhales it. She does this a couple more times before Mela finally takes her first proper breath in what feels like hours. Allison chucks the stuff to the side as she crushes Mela against her chest, both of them clinging to each other. I slump as guilt wars inside me. I nearly killed my daughter because I was pissed off at Allison. She would have died if it wasn't for her! I slowly climb off the bed and run my hand over Mela's head and smile at her.

"I'm so sorry, Mela. I love you, sweet girl." I ignore Allison's gasp as I carry on. "I promise I won't hurt you anymore." Allison looks at me with a questioning stare as I stand straight. "The twins will take you home. I'll pay for everything you and Mela need. I'll cover the tuition for you to go back to college and I'll pay for a nanny for Mela so she doesn't have to go to that school when you have class. You won't have to work again. All you have to do is promise to look after my... daughter and love her like her mother should have." Her eyes are red and puffy from crying. More tears fall and I feel like a piece of shit for tormenting Allison when all she did was love Mela like a mother should.

"King..."

"Don't, Allison. I'll sign whatever papers you need me to. I'll never hurt her again." I take one last look at my little girl who is cuddled against Allison and gripping her shirt for comfort before I turn and walk away.

* * *

Three weeks...

I've just been existing, I haven't felt anything aside from misery and guilt over what I nearly did to my own daughter. One selfish decision nearly cost me the life of my kid. Allison is right! She is so much better off without me, all I do is ruin everything I touch!

"King?" I come out from the library where I have been holed up working out plans to take down another family.

"What?" I snap. Bishop glares at me and I guess I should be grateful he's on my side, the twins come back every weekend with Kiara but they go straight to Allison's and stay there. It pisses me right off, but what did I expect? I pretty much told her to fuck Knight and the thought of them together has my blood boiling!

"You have a visitor. I'm meeting Kiara for dinner so I won't be home tonight." I nod but don't say anything as he heads for the garage. I go to the foyer and screech to a halt when I see Allison standing there looking nervous. I rush forward and grip her arms as panic rises inside me.

"What happened? Is she okay?" She smiles timidly and nods. A whoosh of air escapes me and I nod, taking a step back. I run a hand through my hair as I skim my gaze over her, she looks fucking good in a pair of cut offs that show off her legs and a red crop top that has *DOPE* written across her big tits. I'll admit, I've rubbed more than a dozen out with a picture of her in my mind as I come against my shower wall. Just the thought of her has my cock growing hard. I shake my head to clear my thoughts. "Why are you here, Ally?" Her eyes widen.

"You called me *Ally*?" I furrow my brow in confusion.

"Yeah?" She shrugs her shoulders.

"You've never called me that before." I blow out a frustrated breath.

"Do you need more money or something?" Her eyes blaze with anger.

"No, asshole. I came here to try and talk to you but... forget it." She turns to leave but I snap out and grip her arm hauling back toward me. She steadies herself by placing her hand against my chest, cranes her neck back and flutters her lashes up at me. "King?" she whispers my name like it's a prayer.

"Where's Mela?"

"At home with the twins."

"Why are you here, Allison?" I whisper as I tuck a strand of hair behind her ear. She shivers at my touch and it stirs something inside me to know I can pull that type of reaction from her.

"I-I wanted to see you." I run my fingers through her short hair and grip the back of her neck causing her to gasp. "King, what are you doing?" I can hear the tinge of fear in her voice and I relish in it.

"No one's here, baby. No one is going to come and save you from me." I expect her to scream or fight but she... relaxes.

"What if I don't want to fight?"

"Huh?"

"What if... I'm here to not fight and just because... I kind of... miss you." The feelings I have fought to keep buried for her crash to the surface. I decide to allow myself a moment. She isn't her sister and for some fucked up reason I feel like I can trust her to not go behind my back and fuck one of my brothers to try and get a ring. She hasn't asked me for anything since I sent her away. Rook told me the extra money I put in her account, she has placed in a savings account for Mela. Allison isn't here because of what I can give her, she's here because she just wants... me. She reaches up and wraps her arms around my neck and searches my gaze for a moment before I slowly lower my face to hers, giving her every chance to pull out because if I start this I won't stop.

"Last chance, Ally, stop me now or I'm going to fuck you." Her quiet gasp has my cock hard and ready to ram inside her cunt.

"Do it." I close the space and kiss her. She opens for me and I explore her mouth with my tongue as I run my hands down her sides, I cup her ass and grip it as I lift her. She doesn't break the kiss as I walk us to the closest wall and slam her against it. She moans into my mouth. I pull back and grip her flimsy crop top and tear it from her body. Revealing her tits spilling from the tops of her bra. I reach up and yank one down, her pink nipple is hard and begging me to taste it. I suck it into my mouth and hum my approval when she cries out name. I bite down on it and she screams out, "King." I release her nipple with a pop and hold her gaze as I yank the cup down on the other side and keep my gaze on hers as I suck it into my mouth. I watch as her eyes glaze over in pleasure. "Oh my God."

I move us to the living room, lower her down slowly, then stare down at her. A perfect red blush coats her exposed skin. I reach out and hold her gaze as I undo her pants and slowly pull them and her panties down, groaning at the sight of her bare pussy. I pull my shirt off and chuck it to the side, then push my sweats down and her eyes go wide at the sight of my cock.

"Don't look so scared, baby." She gulps and nods. "Open your legs." She does as I say and the sight of her wet cunt has me groaning. I move to the table in front of her and sit, she sits up and faces me. "Put your feet on the couch and spread your legs wide." She doesn't argue, she does as I ask and I groan as I grip my cock in my hand and stroke it, the sight of her pink pussy has me wanting to blow already. "Touch yourself."

"What?" I smirk at her.

"Don't be shy, baby. Show me how you like it and if you're a good girl I might even eat your cunt before I make you ride my cock." She darts her tongue out to moisten her lips as she slowly reaches down and runs her finger through her folds. A moan escapes her when she circles her clit. "Finger fuck your pussy." She bites her lip as she shakes her head. "Do it!" I order, her eyes blaze with defiance.

"I don't know how!" she shrieks. I stare at her in confusion.

"What do you mean?" She looks away from me but I'm not having it. I lurch forward and nestle myself between her open legs. That has her gaze snapping back to mine. "Explain."

"Christine got pregnant when I was seventeen and Mela was born when I was eighteen so I haven't... there is just not a lot of time... I mean..." My mouth drops open as realization dawns on me.

"You're a virgin?" She cringes and looks away from me. I grip her chin and turn her back to face me. I can see the shame in her eyes and it pisses me off. "Why are you embarrassed about it?" She scoffs.

"Your... you. I shouldn't even want to do this with you because you kill people and yet, here I am wanting to fuck the big bad mafia boss because he makes me wet every time I see him with my niece. There, are you happy now?" I roll my lips between my teeth to stop myself from laughing at her. I cup her face between my hands and kiss her. She doesn't need some quick fuck on the couch for her first time. I wrap my arms around her and lift her, then carry her up the stairs and head for my room. I kick the door closed behind us just in case. She continues to kiss me as I walk us over to the bed. I can feel her wetness on me she grinds up and down needing some friction. I plan to make this experience for her one she will never forget, I'm going to make Allison mine. This will be a night she will never forget a memory that will live inside her beautiful head forever.

Chapter Ten

Allison

He breaks our kiss and lowers me to the bed gently like I'm made of glass. This is a side to King I have never seen before. Normally he is all hard edges and growling at everything I do or glaring at me but, now he is looking at me like he truly sees me for the first time and not the ghost of my sister. I had planned to come here and talk to him about Mela, to try and resolve what happened a few weeks ago, but all thought fled my mind when he touched me. He nestles himself between my legs and I feel his cock brush against my pussy and gasp. He smirks cockily down at me before placing a tender kiss to my lips.

"I'm gonna eat your pussy and make you scream my name, then and only then will I push my cock deep inside your cunt and make you forget that you ever existed in this world without me." His words have me clenching on nothing but air, my pussy has wanted him from the first moment I saw him—it just took my head a while longer to catch up. He slides down my body, rests back on his haunches and gazes down at my wet cunt that is greedy for him to make it feel good. "Fuck, your pussy is beautiful." He doesn't wait for me to respond as he lowers his head down and swipes his tongue up my slit. I buck off the bed and cry out. He grips my hips and holds me in place as he buries his face inside my pussy, making me writhe beneath him and speak in fucking tongues.

"Oh fuck, don't stop." I can feel myself tightening and getting ready to come, I may not have had sex before but I do have a detachable shower head and know how to make myself come. As my body begins to tremble, I reach down and grip his hair, tugging on the strands as I hold his face right where I want it and begin to thrust my hips. I cry out his name as I explode, having the best fucking orgasm of my life! Of course, the mafia King would be the first person to give me the most earth-shattering climax of my life. He scoots back off the bed and grips my ankles yanking me down till my ass balances on the edge of the bed.

"I'm gonna fuck you and then I'm gonna eat that cunt again." His words draw a moan from me. "Your cum is the sweetest fucking thing I have ever tasted. I want it for breakfast, lunch and dinner daily!" He lines his cock up with my entrance and I tense in anticipation. "Relax, baby, it will only hurt for a minute and then I'll make you feel so good." I nod and try do as he says but when he pushes inside me my body locks up. He keeps pushing inside me and it hurts so fucking bad.

"Just do it!" I grit out. He obeys and slams inside me. I feel the moment he shatters the innocence of my childhood, gasping and having tears trek down my cheek. King kisses each of them away and I can see the strain on his face. Him not being able to move inside me while I try to adjust is just as hard for him as it is for me. He kisses me and after a second, I begin to relax and melt back into the mattress. He slowly moves inside me, it stings. After a couple moments the pain turns to bearable, then pleasure begins to thrum through me as I moan into his mouth. He pulls back and smiles down at me, stands tall, grips both my legs and places them over his shoulders. He begins to thrust inside me at a punishing speed and fuck I scream at the feeling. He is making me want to rip my hair out... I can feel myself wanting to explode but I've never done this before. "King?" I moan. He meets my stare and it shocks me to see the glazed over look in his eyes. His gaze is filled with heat as he fucks me like a savage beast.

"Let go, baby, come all over my fucking cock!" His words push me over the edge, I feel my pussy clamp down on his cock as I slam my eyes closed and scream out his name. Ripples of pleasure thrum through my body—I feel weightless and invigorated at the same time. "Fuck yes, I'm gonna come so deep inside your cunt." I open my eyes and try to quiet myself but I can't. I cry out when he hits that sweet spot inside me, reaches down and rubs his thumb over my clit making me moan. "Get there, Allison. I want you to come with me and I'm so close, baby." I do as he demands. Within a couple seconds of him fucking me and stroking my clit I scream his name as he roars out his release and spills jets of his cum deep inside my pussy.

He pushes my legs from his shoulders and drops down on top of me, the only sounds in the room are our ragged breaths. We are both covered in a sheen of sweat, having him pressed against me naked like this has me wanting to stay wrapped up in his arms forever. I reach up and run my fingers through his hair, he turns his face and nuzzles into the side of my neck and a small moan escapes him. I use my other hand to run my nails down his back which causes him to shiver and his cock to jolt inside me which has me gasping. He chuckles into the side of my neck before pulling back and resting his arms either side of my head and capturing my lips in a soft kiss.

"I'm gonna pull out now. It's going to sting like a bitch but I'll run a bath, okay?" I nod as if on autopilot. He slowly pulls out of me and I hiss. Pain etches his features and I can see he hates that he has hurt me, which is funny since he's strangled me a few times and never once said sorry about that. He reaches down and grips my hand in his, pulling me to my feet. The ache between my legs hurts as I follow after him into the bathroom. He lets go of me as he runs a bath and tips some oils into it. I just stand here and watch him go about his business. Okay, fine. I gawk at his perfectly plump ass the whole time. "Come on." I shake my head clearing my thoughts and place my hand in his. He steps into the tub first before reaching out, gripping my waist and lifting me. I squeal in surprise which just causes him to chuckle. He sits behind me and I slowly drop down and sit between his legs, resting my back against his chest. I peek down and am horrified when I see the water turn bloody. I try to jump out but he wraps his arms around me and holds me still.

"King, I'm ruining your bath!" He scoffs.

"Baby, seeing your blood in my bath has my ego soaring to new heights." I feel the blush coat my cheeks and wish I could sink beneath the water and hide. His hold around me tightens and I slowly relax back into him again, close my eyes and savor this surreal moment. I never thought I would end up here. King was the taboo fruit. I swore if he ever found Amelia, I would never fall for him. "Now, I guess you didn't come here for sex?" I snort and immediately cover my face with my hands embarrassed that I just did that. His laughter just makes me want to crawl into a hole and die. Who has sex with someone and then fucking snorts? Me, that's who!

"Stop laughing at me!"

"Okay, but you have to tell me why you came here today?" I tense in his embrace. He runs his hands along my sides and it has the tension fleeing my body.

"I wanted to... make things right," I whisper.

"You didn't do anything wrong, Allison. I fucked up." I shift forward and turn in the bath to face him. He lifts me until I'm straddling his lap and have to rest my hands on his shoulders for balance. I should be embarrassed that my tits are right in his face, but I'm not. With him I feel like I can hand over control and just be... free. His hands grip my waist, they are so big he is nearly able to wrap them around me.

"You didn't fuck up. I shouldn't have lied to you." I take a deep breath and try to explain myself better. "When I found out what Christine had planned with Knight, I pleaded with her to not do it. I mean, I didn't even know you guys then but I still knew it was wrong to do that to any person, even if they are in the mafia. Christine was my sister but she also was a horrible human most of the time. I was with her when she found out she was pregnant. She wanted to abort and I pleaded with her to not do it. A baby is a gift no matter the circumstances and shouldn't have to pay the cost for someone else's actions. Anyway, the night she crashed I made a choice. I live with the guilt of that every day but... I don't regret it." He reaches up and cups my face stroking his thumbs over my cheeks.

"You saved my daughter's life. You made the right choice, Allison. Christine and I were toxic together. We should never have lasted as long as we did, but no matter what I said or did to her, she kept coming back. In the end, it was just convenience." His words ring true.

"I'm sorry about what happened with your brother." His eyes harden for a second before he asks.

"Have you and... Knight?" I gasp and glare down at him.

"I was a virgin until like ten minutes ago, jackass!"

"You don't need to fuck to come," he snaps angrily. I take a deep breath and count to three to tamper my anger.

"No. Knight has been nothing but a good friend. Rook is... Rook." That draws a light chuckle from him. "Look, I think Knight has been around so much because he feels like he owes something to Amelia for what happened to her mom." His eyes search mine for a beat.

"You're her mom." I reel back in shock and shake my head.

"I... I'm not." He leans forward and places a tender kiss to my lips.

"You are her mother in every sense of the word, Ally. She loves you and clings to you like a child would their mother. She may have birthed her, but you have been there. You know her needs and wants. You raised the most incredible fucking kid and I am indebted to you." His words have tears leaking from my eyes. I didn't know how much I wanted someone to say that to me until he did. I've loved Amelia as my own since the day she was handed to me. I kiss him and try to show him without words how much that meant to me for him to say that.

"You need to come see her," I whisper against his lips. He closes his eyes and shakes his head.

"I can't..."

"Why not?"

"I nearly killed her, Allison!" he snaps angrily. I cup his face and stare into his eyes.

"No. She has asthma, King. All kids get sick and it's scary as fuck, but that wasn't your fault. She got overwhelmed and that's all there is to it."

"I didn't know what to do. I froze like an idiot."

"Shhh. I'll teach you but she really wants to see her daddy." His eyes widen in shock as he stares up at me.

"You... you told her?" I bit my lip and nod. "When?"

"The night after we left here. She had questions and I swore I would never lie to her if she asked."

"Is... does she hate me?" The anguish in his voice breaks my heart.

"No, she just doesn't understand why you have disappeared. She needs you, King. You can buy her the world and it will mean nothing to her. She just wants you to be present and love her. I've seen the way you are with her. I've watched you watch her, and I can see the love you have for her in your eyes—just her name has a sparkle entering your eyes." A slow smile spreads across his face.

"I don't want to fuck it up with her. My parents.. .they weren't good. I don't know how to be better." I cover his mouth with mine cutting off his tirade. When I pull back, I smirk and say,

"Now, that shut you up." He tickles my sides and has me sloshing water over the edge of the bath as I plead for mercy. My laughter dies when he sucks my nipple into his mouth. As if my body knows what to do I grind down on his hard cock and gasp. He releases my nipple with a pop and stares up at me with lust in his green eyes.

"Are you too sore?" I shake my head, the need for him inside me is outweighing the pain.

"I need you." Those three little words have him snapping into action and positioning me so I'm hovering over the top of his cock.

"Slide down on me, baby." I do as he says as he cups my tits in each of his hands. As I slowly sink down on his cock, a hiss escapes me but I don't stop. My pussy slowly stretches to accommodate his size, both of us panting and thrumming with need by the time his cock is buried inside me. I grip the edges of the tub as I slowly rock back and forward on his cock. Water spills over the edges but neither of us give a shit. We keep our gazes on each other as I ride him. He rolls my nipples between his fingers and I throw my head and moan. "Fuck, Ally, you feel so good." I stare back down at him, my eyes hazy with need.

"I... I need more." He nods and lifts me off him.

"Stand up and bend over... Grip the edge of the tub and hold on tight." I do as he says. I hear him move behind me, then he grips my hips in a punishing hold, and slams into me. I cry out in part pleasure and pain. "Fuck, your pussy fits my cock like a glove, baby."

"King, fuck me hard." He obeys, slamming his hips into me over and over again until I scream his name. His hold on me is the only thing keeping me up.

"I'm gonna come, baby. Take my cum deep inside that cunt."

"Fuck, yes! I want every drop of it inside me," I shout, my body still shaking from the aftershocks of my release as he slams one last time inside me, crying out my name as he comes inside me for the second time.

Chapter Eleven

King

Nervous energy thrums through me as I pull up outside Allison's. After fucking her in the bath, we decided a shower was in order. I tore her shirt, so she's wearing one of mine and knotted it in the front. I like the look of her in my clothes. Every time I look at her now my cock is instantly hard. I would have never guessed she was a fucking virgin! She did more than drop out of school for Amelia, she gave up her life to raise *my* kid. Knowing she never had guys around my girl has me grinning. I climb out of the car and release a nervous breath. I meet Allison on the path and grip her hand in mine as I lead her up the stairs. I know it's late but I couldn't wait till tomorrow to see my little girl. Allison leads us toward the door of her apartment but I pause. I turn in a slow circle, looking up and down the street as I can feel eyes on me. I grip her hand tighter and pull her into the building. She says nothing as I lead her up the stairs. I pull my key from my pocket and unlock the door, ignoring her chuckle as I push it open. The twins and Amelia are sitting on the couch. Rook jumps to his feet and points at Knight.

"I didn't give her the candy, I told him not to." Knight smacks Rook's hand away and glares at his twin.

"Why aren't you two at school?" Both of them look to Allison. I turn and peer down at her but then get distracted by her melodic voice.

"Daddy!" Everything inside me freezes as I turn back toward the couch and watch as Amelia jumps to her feet. Chocolate is smeared all over her mouth and her eyes are blown wide from her sugar rush. She races toward me and I drop to my knees as she launches herself into my arms. I hold her tightly against my chest. I can feel the twins staring but ignore them. Allison sniffles beside me but my only focus is on my little girl and the fact that she called me *daddy!*

"We'll get out of here and give you both... some time." I look up to my brothers and watch as each of them hugs Allison and kisses her cheek goodbye. She promises to call them tomorrow. I know she doesn't view them that way, but knowing her sister fucked Knight behind my back, has my jealousy rearing inside me. Mela pulls back and plants a wet kiss to my cheek that has me fucking *blushing*. I don't blush!

"I missed you." A smile spreads across my face. I run my hands all over her face.

"I missed you too, baby girl."

"You my daddy?"

"Yeah, baby, I am." She nods and I can see the cogs in her mind turning.

"All the bad gone now?" Her question throws me. Allison kneels down beside me with a scornful look on her face.

"Not yet, Meelz, you should be in bed!" Mela smiles sheepishly.

"Uncle Cook and Uncle Right let me watch the toons." Allison sighs and shakes her head.

"I'll be having words to them. Now kiss your daddy goodnight and let's get you to bed."

"Actually, pack a bag." Mela squeals and races off to her room. Allison stares at me with worry lines marrying her face.

"What's wrong?"

"I changed my mind. You can't stay here anymore." Her brows pull together in confusion.

"Why not? This is our home, King."

"Because, it isn't safe here, Ally. I know you don't like what I am and what I do but her being my daughter makes her a target and you're being followed. I need you both to stay with me for a while until we can sort something else out." I expect her to argue and fight me on this.

"Okay. If it keeps Mela safe, I'll pack some things now."

We pull up to the house and I spot Knight's Dodge in the driveway. I look back and smile at Amelia snoring softly in her seat. I turn back to Allison and ask the question that has been burning in my mind since we arrived at her apartment.

"Why are my brothers at your apartment and not school?" She bites her lips and twists her hands in her lap.

"I went to the store the other day and I thought someone was following me..."

"Why didn't you call me?" She flinches away from me and I berate myself for being an ass. She faces me and I can see the challenge in her blue eyes.

"Really? Three days ago you weren't exactly on the best terms with me. I came here today to talk about Mela *and* to tell you about it but it slipped my mind after..."

"I fucked you?" I supply and a blush coats her cheeks as she nods. "I'll figure it out, okay?"

"Okay."

"Until then, you both stay here with me."

"Look, just because we had sex, I don't expect you to move me in. I know you need to do this for Mela but..." I grip the back of her neck and haul her half way across the console, then smash my lips against hers. The fight drains from her and I moan into her mouth. The taste of her has my cock rock fucking hard and wanting inside her again. I pull back and rest my head against hers.

"Let's put our girl to bed and then I'm gonna fuck you until you pass out." I feel her shiver against me and relish the way her body responds to its master.

I sit on the edge of the bed and stare down at her naked form, then run a hand through my hair as I reach over and grip my phone. I scroll through the contacts until I find Bishop's number and hit dial, it rings a few times before he answers.

"What happened?"

"It's the Ramello's." I can hear him shuffling around on the other end of the phone before he answers.

"What did they do?"

"Someone's tailing Allison. She called the twins to come

stay because she thought someone had followed her a couple days ago."

"I know, I told Mav to put four guys on watch." I grip my phone so tight I think it might break.

"And you didn't fucking tell me?" I whisper shout, not wanting to wake Allison.

"You've been fucking avoiding me for days. If I so much as mention her fucking name, you lose your shit! I did what I had to do to ensure my family remained safe, so fuck off with your bullshit, King!" Hearing him refer to Allison and not just Mela as family has my respect and my love for my brother growing.

"Thank you," I whisper.

"Don't thank me, dumbass. They're family and we always watch out for our own. It isn't the Ramello's trailing her." That has me sitting up straight.

"How do you know?"

"Look, I'll fill you in tomorrow. I got a girl to fuck and I'm pretty sure there is blonde beside you right now, so fuck off and go annoy her." I chuckle as he ends the call. Bishop knows me better than I give him credit for, that is for damn sure.

Chapter Twelve

Allison

Three weeks...

Mela and I have been staying here with King—the twins and Kiara are on break from school and back home. My days are spent hanging out with the twins and Mela, sometimes Kiara as well when she isn't doing Bishop all hours of the day. Rook splashes water in my face and I turn to glare at him. It's such a beautiful day and it's rare to get a nice warm day like this so close to winter, so we decided to swim. Knight is teaching Mela to swim beside us and I have to say I think he is her favorite.

"What's your plans for Christmas?"

"What do you mean?" Rook rolls his eyes at me.

"Do you have any traditions that you do?" I smile and nibble on my lip as I swim over to the side.

"I take Mela to look at the lights and we bake cookies for Santa and watch *Home Alone* every Christmas Eve."

"Awww, that actually sounds fun." He slings his arm over my shoulder and draws me into his side. "This year, you won't be doing that shit alone with Meelz, we'll be here with you both." He has no idea how much that means to me. It's always just been Mela and me.

"You're the best, thank you, Rook." I place a kiss to his cheek and smile at him.

"So, you're fucking the other twin?" Rook and I spin around to see King standing at the end of the pool glaring at us. I open my mouth to deny his claim and defend myself but what's the point? King constantly makes snide remarks, glares or scowls at me whenever I speak to the twins or hang out with them. I've done nothing wrong! I lift myself onto the edge and hop out. I don't have the energy to fight with him daily. Don't get me wrong, the make-up sex is fucking amazing but I can't live like this. I grab my towel off the lounger and wrap it around my waist as I head inside. Just as I pass King, he reaches out and grips my arm halting my exit. I glare up at him and try to yank free of his hold but he's so much bigger and stronger than I am. "Answer me!" he growls right in my face.

"What do you want me to say?" I snap, keeping my voice low so Mela doesn't hear.

"The fucking truth. Are you screwing my brother?" I've had enough of his accusations, I hear Rook scoff behind us.

"Which one, King? Every day you accuse me of screwing one of them so who is it today? It was Knight yesterday, so is it Bishop or Rook? Cause, you know Bishop comes knocking every day after he fucks Kiara first." At the sound of a throat clearing I turn to the side and see Bishop and Kiara walking toward us from the pool house. Kiara is trying not to laugh but Bishop looks murderous.

"You seriously think, I would fucking do that to you?" I can hear the threat in Bishop's tone, King is treading on thin ice here. Kiara reaches up and places her hand on Bishop's chest trying to calm him, her blue diamond sparkles in the afternoon sunlight.

"Daddy, look me." It grates on my nerves more than him accusing me of cheating when he ignores Mela. I yank my arm free and step back. His eyes bore into mine as I shake my head, so tired of this same argument.

"I'm not my fucking sister!" I scream at him, all the emotions I have buried come crashing to the surface after weeks of pushing them down. "You can fucking treat me how you want, but you do not get to ignore my daughter!" My eyes widen as soon as the word flees from my mouth. Much like a movie, everything around me goes deathly silent, not a word is uttered as everyone, including me, waits to see how King will react to my claim on Amelia. He closes the space between us, grips the back of my neck and places a chaste kiss to my lips before pulling back. His eyes shine with disgust and loathing, I know what comes out of his mouth next is going to be a blow to my fucking heart.

"That was cute, but let's not forget you're just her glorified aunt who is playing mommy." Tears prick my eyes at his cruel words. I hear someone get out of the pool behind me but I can't pull my gaze from him to check. Knight shoots past me and punches King right across the jaw. He stumbles back a step but launches at Knight, tackling him to the ground. Bishop tries to stop them but can't. Rook jumps out of the pool and tries to help his oldest brother. Kiara jumps in to help them but Knight and King are rolling along the ground punching each other and trading blow for blow.

"Fucking stop!" Rook shouts, but they don't listen. Bishop grabs the back of King's shirt but it tears away when he pulls. Kiara is trying to help Rook get Knight but–the sounds of splashes draws my attention and that's when my whole world crashes down. Mela is upside down in her floaty ring, her legs kicking in the air while her head is in the water.

"Amelia!" I scream as I run and jump in the pool swimming for her. My heart is racing inside my chest as I swim as fast as I can to get to my baby. I hear someone else jump in the water just as I reach her and tip her the right way. She gasps and splutters water out as she screams for me. I pull her out of her ring and tap her back as I move toward the steps. Bishop tries to help me with Mela but I turn and drop down on the edge of the pool with her in my arms. Her cries break me. I keep tapping her back as she coughs and cries for me. "I'm right here, baby," I choke out and cry with her. When she finally stops coughing, I crush her against me and climb to my feet. King launches himself out of the pool and all five of them stand in front of me.

"Allison—" I pin King with a look.

"Don't you dare, don't you fucking dare! I'm taking Mela and we are leaving. You so much as try and stop me I will fucking shoot you with your own gun!" Pain shines in his eyes. Knight steps forward and I just stare at him.

"Ally, I'm so sorry. I didn't..."

"Knight, stop. I can't do this right now. I'm gonna pack our things and then you can tell me about it on the way to dropping us off?" He nods and steps aside. I keep my head high as I walk past them, knowing I probably just signed my own death warrant but I can't be here. Mela nearly fucking died! I take the steps two at a time as I make my way to King's room to pack our things. I knew this was a bad idea. I can't believe I was so stupid! I go into the bathroom and grab a towel to wrap around Mela, sit her on the edge of the bed, then kneel down in front of her and rub her arms. Silent tears leak from her eyes. I place a kiss to her forehead and will my tears to remain at bay. "Stay right here." I leave her on the edge of the bed as I grab our bags and start pulling clothes from the hangers and shoving them in the bags. As I walk out of the closet with one of the bags, I spot King in the doorway. He looks so torn but I don't have the emotional capacity to deal with his shit right now.

"I'm sorry." I scoff as I place the bag next to Mela and check her again. I need to keep an eye on her for silent drowning.

"Is she okay?" I look over my shoulder and nod to Knight, he and King stand stiffly beside each other. Knight moves toward me but King snaps out his arm stopping him. Knight turns to his brother and the remorseful look on his face tells me he didn't mean for the fight to get out of hand.

"You stay the fuck away from my family." I gasp.

"No, you do not get to do that." King swings his angry gaze to me—Rook, Bishop and Kiara now stand behind the guys and my frustration grows at the sight of all of them. "Knight hasn't done a thing to me or Mela. Your own jealousy and the fact you can't get past what my sister did is ruining us!"

"It's you not her—" My pent-up anger snaps. I march over to him and stop only leaving a couple of inches of space between us.

"You blame me for Christine!" I stop myself for a second. I don't take my eyes off King as I speak to Knight. "Take Mela and do not take your eyes off her for a second.

I'll meet you both downstairs." Knight moves toward Mela and King tries to follow but I stop him with a hand against his chest. Knight strolls past us a moment later and Rook follows after them. Bishop and Kiara stand in the doorway awkwardly but I don't care, I need to get this shit off my chest.

"You are not taking my daughter." I shove his chest but he doesn't budge and it pisses me off more.

"Fuck you! I am taking her away from you and your house of horrors. I knew this was a mistake bringing her here. She isn't safe with you. I was stupid to think it was because of your association with the mafia and what you do for your family. It isn't, it's you who is fucking toxic. You are taking out your anger toward my sister on me. I never coerced your thirteen-year-old brother to have his way with me. I never mentally fucked him up. *I* would never do that, but my sister did!" His eyes widen at my omission but I push on, I can feel Kiara and Bishop staring at me like I've lost my mind, maybe I have. "I'm not Christine, King. Until you realize that and sort out your shit, I am taking Mela with me and we are going home where she will be safe from you and all your bullshit. You need help, so does Knight, but you men are too proud to admit that." He reaches out to grab me but I step out of reach and shake my head. "I won't be your punching bag anymore," I whisper.

"Allison—" Kiara cuts King off.

"I'll take you home and stay with you." We all turn to her in shock. "Gage, the twins and I will stay with you."

"Like fuck. You aren't going anywhere!" It's the first time I've heard Bishop speak to her like that and it shocks me when she melts and smiles up at him with so much love in her eyes.

"Bish, you know I'm going with her even if you say no.

Come on, let's go pack me a bag and I'll call Gage." She grips his hand and leads him from the room.

"That little bitch isn't staying with you!" he grumbles. Kiara just laughs and drags him after her. King and I stand here staring at each other. I see him in a whole different light now. I allowed his sweet words and beauty to fool me into a false sense of security. I thought that I could be a part of his life if I ignored what he did for a living and I did. It isn't his job as Bishop's underboss that has me wanting to leave, it's how treats me daily!

"You're not taking my daughter!" he speaks the words quietly but they have so much weight to them.

"I'll leave her here with you if you can answer me three things." He nods like the cocky fucker he is. "When's her birthday?" He narrows his eyes at me and grinds his teeth. I open my mouth to answer but he cuts me off.

"Thirtieth of May, 2018." That shocks the fuck out of me, honestly. I kind of expected him to know but wasn't a hundred percent sure he actually knew.

"What's her favorite color?" He flicks his gaze away from me and I know I have him. "Last question, what is Amelia's middle name?" That has his gaze swinging back to me. I can see in his gaze he is pissed he doesn't know the answer but I also know he wants me to tell him the answers, but won't. I turn my back on him and grab the other bag from the closet. I snag one of his shirts from the hanger and pull it over my swim suit, grab the other bag off the bed and don't spare him a glance as I make my way past him.

"Allison?" I stop right on the threshold but don't turn to face him.

"What, King?" I hate that I can hear the heartache in my own voice, it is taking everything inside me not to break down and cry right now.

"I'm sorry I'm such a fuck up. I don't deserve you." I steel my spine and shake my head.

"You may not deserve me now, but the thing is you could. You need help, King, and I don't think I am the one to give it to you. I can't be. I'm already raising a child and I sure as shit never agreed to mother you as well. Come see her whenever you want. I'll be getting a new bank account so please, stop sending money."

"No, Allison..." I push on needing to get this out before I cry.

"I don't want your money, we aren't together, King. I'm not your problem. You can still do things for Mela though." I take another step away from him and feel like my heart is about to shatter inside my chest and pause. "For what it's worth, I think you are a good man, King, and I really wish we could have worked out." I don't wait for a reply as I head downstairs and away from the man that I now know owns my heart.

Chapter Thirteen

Allison

The ride back to my place is filled with silence. I rest my head against the window and close my eyes. Knight drives—Kiara, Rook and Amelia are in the backseat. Knight reaches across and interlaces his fingers with mine, giving it a small squeeze. His kind gesture is what breaks the flood gates. I burst into tears. No one in the car utters a single word, not even Mela, as I break down and cry. My heart is breaking. I think I always knew from the moment King first kissed me that he would have the power to obliterate my heart. Knight holds my hand the whole way to my house. When we pull up out front, I wipe away my tears with my free hand and take a deep breath. I need to pull myself together. I cannot allow Mela to see me break like this. I'll cry myself to sleep tonight if I have to.

We all climb out of the car and grab our bags from the back. I lift Mela into my arms and hold her close to me and just breath in her scent. I came so close to losing her today and that is a loss I would never survive... Instead, I just lost her father and I don't know if that is a loss I will ever recover from either. Rook wraps an arm around me as he leads me up the stairs. We come to a halt when Kiara squeals, and all turn to watch her take off down the sidewalk toward a man dressed in ripped jeans and an old rock band shirt. His blond hair is tied in a man bun atop his head—his green eyes sparkle with joy at the sight of the black-haired beauty charging toward him.

"Who is that?" I ask Rook. He sighs and shakes his head.

"That is off limits to you, babe. He already coped a broken hand for touching Kiara." I lift my gaze to him in surprise.

"You're joking?" He shakes his head as Knight comes to stand on my other side.

"He isn't, unless you want to bury his body. I suggest you stay clear of him because King won't hesitate to take him out if you so much as make fuck me eyes at him." I balk at Knight.

"I-I wasn't." I try to defend myself. I won't lie, the man is fucking gorgeous, anyone with eyes can see that. He has that rugged beauty and it's effortless. He seems like the type to not even know just how good looking he is.

"Yeah, and Rook wasn't checking out your tits in the pool." My mouth drops in shock. Rook chuckles and shoves Knight.

"Snitch." Really? Rook doesn't even deny his twin's claim.

"Come on, if we don't see them making out then Bishop

can't blame us for killing Gage." I follow after the twins. Knight talks about killing that man like it means nothing. I don't think I will ever get used to how this family operates and how they can end a life without second thought.

———

One week,

I'm about to lose my fucking mind!

The twins are slobs. Gage just sits in the corner looking out the window all day every day. Kiara comes and goes as she visits Bishop I clean all day, every day and I'm about over it. I need a fucking break from the chaos these three wreck on my apartment daily! I have tried to get them to leave, begged even, but they just laugh. I even asked Bishop to help. He told me I brought it upon myself and I have to deal with it on my own. As I walk into the lounge and see Rook hand Mela a soda, I turn on my heel and storm back into my room slamming the door. I grab my phone off the bed and scroll through my contacts until I find his number, it rings for so long I fear he won't answer, until he does.

"Allison." The sound of his voice is like a balm to my tattered nerves. Just hearing my name come from his lips has my body wired.

"I need your help." I hear him mutter to someone and then a door close before he answers.

"What's wrong? Where are you?" I blow out a frustrated breath.

"I need you to get the twins out and take fucking Gage with you. I can't do it anymore!" I'm so exhausted from trying to clean and job hunt as well as chasing Mela daily that I just need some fucking peace! When I hear his laughter on the other end of the phone, I lose it. "You know what, screw you. I should never have called!" I end the call and chuck my phone on the bed. I decide to leave the twins to deal with Mela's sugar high and take a shower, I don't even know when the last time I had one was. I only have a two-bedroom apartment and the three guys sleep on the sofa's. Mela has been sleeping with me and Kiara has her room when she stays. I spend a generous amount of time in the shower as I wash my hair and shave everywhere, my legs look like a fucking yeti's fur. I've had no need to maintain myself since I have no one to impress. I exit the bathroom and storm back into my room with my towel wrapped around me, kick the door shut and drop my towel but freeze at the sight in front of me.

"Don't stop on my account, baby." I scramble to pick my towel up and quickly wrap it around me again.

"What are you doing here?" My eyes drink in the sight of him, reclined back on my bed with his ankles crossed. His black jeans hug him in just the right way, his arms resting behind his head causing his biceps to bulge in the right way, his white shirt taut across his chest in the right way. His dual colored hair is a mess atop his head but his eyes, those forest green eyes have my body heating just from the way he stares at me like he owns every inch of me.

"You called, I came." His words shouldn't have me feeling giddy but they do. I decide we need to have this conversation when I'm not practically naked so I head for my drawers. I grab out a pair of panties and half scream, half shriek when they are yanked from my hand. I spin around and slam back against my dresser in fright. King stands there holding my black lace panties, my eyes track his movements as he balls them up in his hand and lifts them to his nose inhaling, my mouth drops open in shock but I can also feel myself getting wet over the sight of him sniffing my panties. "These would have smelt sweeter if you had just peeled them off." I stand here dumfounded as I stare up him, I'm at a loss for words. He stuffs my panties into his back pocket before resting his arms on either side of me, caging me in.

I hold his gaze as he slowly leans down and runs his nose along my collarbone and up to my neck. He sucks my flesh into his mouth and drags a moan from me. I bite down on my lip to silence myself, he licks up my neck and then sucks my lobe into his mouth. I'm a fucking panting mess now. He moves his hand down and yanks my towel open. I don't even stop him when I know I should. He runs his index finger down my chest and over my nipple causing me to shudder and a satisfied smirk crosses his face as he continues to run his digit down my stomach. He cups my pussy and I jerk back, causing the dresser to rattle behind me, and gasp. He sucks on the other side of my neck as he swipes his finger through my lips. I moan when he runs the top of his finger over my clit, and slowly rubs it before going lower, plunging his finger inside me.

"Fuck, you're so fucking wet for me, baby."

"Hmmm." Is my only response. I reach out and grip the tops of his shoulders to steady myself as he pushes in and out of me and I stifle my moans by biting down on my lip.

"You like that, baby?" I rest my head against his shoulder.

"Yes."

"You want me to make you come on my fucking finger?"

"God, yes!"

"Then can I fuck you?" I feel my orgasm building and begin to ride his fucking hand like my life depends on it.

"Yes!"

"Good." He yanks his hand back and pulls away from me. I stare at him confused and horny as fuck. He slips his finger into his mouth and moans at the taste of me. I stand here like an idiot and just watch transfixed on the sight in front of me. "You taste so good."

"Why did you stop?" I sound like a wanton slut but I was right fucking there, ready to come all over his hand and let him fuck me however he wanted! And, he left me hanging!

"You hurt my feelings so, I'm going to hurt your cunt as payback!" I gape at the audacity of him.

"I hurt your feelings?" His eyes gleam with want, I can tell from the way he is fighting to keep his gaze on mine that he wants me. I do the boldest thing I have ever done in my life. I waltz past him, making sure to sway my hips side to side, and crawl onto the bed. I can feel his gaze on my ass and my exposed pussy. I turn around and lean against the headboard and slowly spread my legs open. His gaze is laser focused on my every move. I cup my breasts and arch my back... When I pinch my nipples, a zing of awareness shoots through me. I keep my gaze on his as I slide my hands down my body and rub my inner thighs before parting my pussy. A hiss escapes him at the sight. I slide a finger through my slick folds and moan, then use one hand to circle my clit and my other hand to sink two fingers inside my dripping cunt.

"Allison..." I can hear the warning in his tone but I don't give a fuck, he denied me my orgasm and with or without him I'm going to come. In fact, having him watch me finger fuck myself is the hottest thing I have ever seen. Thanks to him I now know what I like and how I like it. I pull my fingers out and continue to circle my clit as I lift my fingers to my mouth, suck them clean, then moan at the taste of my own arousal. He growls, spins toward the door, making my heart sink thinking he is about to leave. He opens the door and calls out, "Take Mela for ice cream, you have five seconds to get the fuck out now!" My face burns, they are all going to know what we are doing in here. He closes the door and turns back to me smirking. "Don't get all shy on me now, baby. You got my attention, so keep going." I continue to play with my clit as I speak.

"You're not fucking me... You can watch but you're not touching." His eyes narrow to slits, a growl sounds out and I smirk before a breathy moan tears from me. He yanks his shirt off, kicks his shoes off next and then pops the button on his jeans and slowly slides them down his muscular legs.

Chapter Fourteen

King

The sight of her all flushed and exposed to me has my cock springing free and slapping against my stomach. Her eyes drink in the sight of me as I grip the base of my cock and pump, a small hiss escaping me as I watch her plunge two fingers inside her tight, wet cunt. Her eyes are hazy and filled with need and I refuse to help her out until she begs me for it. She turned my fucking world upside down when she left. I've thrown myself into work this past week and barely slept a wink. I facetime Amelia everyday thanks to Rook but I miss having my girls with me daily and I know I fucked up. The sound of her moans has me focusing back on her. I know her tiny fingers won't be able to reach that sweet spot that I can. My cock aches in my hand but there is no way I'm blowing my load in my hand when I have her perfect pink pussy staring right at me. I'm coming inside that cunt!

"You like that, baby?" Her eyes lazily flick to me.

"It feels so fucking good." Her voice is breathy and it's starting to make me impatient that she hasn't given in yet and asked me to bring her to climax.

"You gonna come?" My voice sounds rough and husky.

"Yes, fuck I'm gonna come so hard—"

"On your hand?" I cut in. She pulls her hand free and drops her arms to her sides and stares at me with nothing but... love?

"No, King. You're going to make me come at least a dozen times before Mela and the twins get back and then you and I are going to sit down and talk shit out." I open my mouth to cut in but she carries on. "Get the fuck over here and bury your face in my pussy!" Fuck me side ways, this girl was made for me.

"Yes, ma'am." I don't need to be told twice, fuck making her beg. I need to taste her and then bury my cock inside her. It's been a fucking week and I need this... we both need this. I don't fuck around. I suck her clit into my mouth as I pump two fingers inside her. She screams out my name and I hope to God that the twins and Mela have gone.

"Fuck, yes. Just like that!" I keep up my relentless pace and finger fuck the shit out of her whilst licking her clit like a lollipop. "I'm gonna come, don't stop, please." I don't, not this time. She cries out her release as her pussy clenches my fingers. I don't bring her down from her high, instead I sit back, line my cock up with her entrance and push inside. Her back arches off the bed as she cries out, while I groan at the feeling of being inside her again. It feels like home. I reach down and grip the back of her neck, pulling her up until she is straddling my lap and kiss her. I pour all my feelings into this kiss. She grips my face and deepens the kiss as she grinds down on my cock. I groan into her mouth as she starts to bounce on my cock, I pull back and stare up at her.

"Fuck you feel so good, baby. I missed your pussy."

"I missed you." Her honestly baffles me for a moment but then she grinds on my cock and I moan.

"You love my cock, don't you?" She holds my gaze as she slows her rhythm and cups my face.

"No, I love you." Her words have me stilling beneath her, even though she doesn't stop riding me. She doesn't overreact that I don't say a thing, instead she kisses me and brings me back to the moment. I grip her hips and lift her before slamming her back down on my cock. Next thing I know, we're both screaming out the other's name as we reach our climax together, as one.

***

Allison and I both sit on the sofa that has the twins shit and Gage's shirt, along with Mela's toys scattered all around us. Allison stands and begins to start clearing up the soda cans and the empty pizza boxes. I stand and follow after her. She tries to brush past me in the kitchen but I block her escape. She sighs and her shoulders droop slightly.

"Can we not do this?" she mumbles. I grip her chin and lift until her eyes meet mine. I hate that I can see sadness in her eyes knowing that I am the cause of it.

"We are doing this. I won't say those words back to you, Allison, until I can be worthy of it. You told me to sort my shit out and I'm trying to, baby. You can walk away a hundred times and you will still belong to me. I nearly fucking shot Gage when the fucker sent me a picture of you bending over picking Mela up!" She gasps.

"King, I swear I have never—" I place a finger against her lips silencing her.

"I know, baby. The twins and Gage have been doing shit all week to fuck with me hoping to push me over the edge."

"Why didn't you... do something about it?"

"Because, someone I care about told me I need to trust them not to be like the snake I used to know from my past." Her eyes fill with tears at my omission. "I am going to fuck this up, baby. I need you to be patient with me, okay?" She smiles wide and sniffs.

"You mean take things... slow?"

"Uh, yeah. I guess." She nods smiling wide and steps back out of my hold and extends her hand toward me. I stare at it. "The fuck are you doing?" She rolls her eyes.

"We're starting over so, hi, I'm Allison and I have a four-year-old kid who is fucking amazing and needs a dad to be added to her birth certificate." My brows jump up in surprise, then guilt slams into me as I place my hand in hers.

"I'm King and I'm about to get kicked in the dick." She laughs and shakes her head.

"Why? Because you went behind my back and got a DNA sample off Mela to change the birth certificate without me?" Now, that shocks the fuck out of me.

"How... did you know?" She shrugs her shoulders and brushes past me as the door opens and the twins, Gage and Mela walk through. Allison twirls around in a circle and flicks her eyes to Knight and Rook, fucking son of bitch! Those assholes are supposed to be loyal to me not... my girl.

"Daddy!" I smile as Mela struggles in Gage's hold to get down. He places her on her feet and she takes off toward me. I crouch down and scoop her up before tossing her in the air. She laughs and it warms everything inside me to hear it. I hug her to me and breathe her in. I spy Allison and the guys all staring at me but I don't care. I may be the underboss but my little girl is the only one who can bring me to my fucking knees.

I sit in Bishop's office and smile down at the photo Allison sent me of her and Mela at the park. She's enrolled in online classes for nursing and I'm fucking proud of her! She has set goals for herself and is smashing them out of the park. We haven't had one fight in four weeks and it feels fucking great. The only part I hate is that she said she won't move in here with me. She wants to take things slow and not fuck them up. She's right though, it's a lot for Mela to deal with, all the coming and going.

"What are you smiling at?" I hand my phone to Bishop. He stares down at the screen and smiles wide. Bishop may not spend as much time with my girl as the twins, and even fucking Gage is always at Allison's now, but I know he loves her. He has taken on more shit lately because I've been spending so much time with Mela and Allison. "They coming round for Christmas?" I smile like a douche and nod.

"Yeah. Kiara and Ally want us to do movie night and smores on Christmas Eve." Bishops scrubs a hand down his face. "Don't fucking act like you will say no to anything Kiara says." He glares at me and I laugh.

"Shut the fuck up. You don't say no to Allison either!"

"Yes, the fuck I do!" He stares at me in utter disbelief.

"How?" I throw my head back and laugh. I never would have thought that the Don of the Murdoch family would ever ask me for advice on how to say no to his fiancée. "Fuck up, asshole!" I take a second to compose myself before answering him.

"Just say no, it's that easy," Bishop scoffs.

"Then I don't get fucking laid!"

"Dude, all you got to do is get naked in front of her and walk into the shower. I bet you your Tesla that Kiara follows you and gets on her knees making it up to you." He eyes me for a beat.

"Deal." I rub my hands together like a child.

"I'm getting a Tesla for Christmas!" I shout. Bishop's phone rings cutting off our conversation, he answers and puts it on speaker.

"Yeah."

"Boss, we got a problem." Mav sounds worried and that is never a fucking good thing.

"What is it?"

"You need to get down to the docks now. We have an hour tops before this gets out." Bishop ends the call and we're both racing out the door to meet Mav and find out what the fuck is going on.

Horror.
Fear.
Anger.

That is the only way I am able to explain how I felt seeing what I did. Bodies of girls my own daughters age and no older than twelve were inside a container wearing next to nothing. They had all been executed. I never lose my cool on a job but both Bishop and I did. We ordered our men to hunt down Mike Ramello and get back to us with his location. Ramello had this container delivered to us in the hopes the feds would find it before we did. That son of a bitch is still in the skin trade even after Bishop put out the order. I turn to Bishop who is white knuckling the steering wheel.

"They still working for the Russians?"

"Yeah, and he isn't the only one. We need to bring Anthony in on this." Fuck, for Bishop to even consider asking Kiara's father for anything that must mean he really does want this shit shut down.

"We'll burn each and every one of their families to the ground until we own New York."

"We start this war, we have to pull everyone back in."

"Fuck!"

"I can't risk it, King. We can deal with the New York families but if we go after the Russians we need the twins and Kiara home. Allison and Mela need to move and... I have to bring Carlina home." Just thinking about my sister has me feeling like a piece of shit.

"Have you heard from her?" He shakes his head.

"She's changed her hair and wears contacts now. She's backpacking with some guy through Amsterdam." A part of me envies my sister and how she was able to run from our family and the toll it takes on you being a Murdoch. She more than paid her fucking dues though. My phone rings and I pull it out. I smile when I see the caller ID and answer.

"Hey, baby—"

"Daddy?" My blood freezes.

"Mela, what's wrong?" I feel Bishop's gaze on me and tell him to go straight to Allison's. He plants his foot.

"Daddy, I scared." My heart lurches into my throat.

"Where's your... Ally?"

"I in the bed. Ally told me to shush and hide, then call

Daddy." Fear like I have never felt before courses through me. I take a deep breath and try to reign in my temper and fear.

"Is... Ally there, baby girl?" The sound of her quiet cries on the other end of the phone kill me. Bishop places a hand on my shoulder offering me comfort but it does nothing. Dread is pooling inside. Bishop pulls his phone out and calls Rook I assume.

"Daddy, I want my mommy." Fuck me, my heart shatters inside my chest that I wasn't there to protect her. My daughter is hiding under Allison's bed, scared out of her mind.

"I'm coming, baby," I choke out. "Just stay there and be quiet, okay? Daddy is coming, baby. I swear, nothing is going to happen to you or your... mom."

Chapter Fifteen

King

I keep Amelia on the phone with me the whole time, her softs cries will forever haunt me. We pull up outside Allison's apartment just as two SUV's come from the opposite direction. I don't wait for Bishop or my brothers as I jump out of the car. I ignore Bishop's shouts as I race through the door and up the stairs praying to God that I don't open her apartment and find her... body. I won't recover from losing Allison, she is my fucking heart, my soul, my purpose! I love her as much as I love Mela and I will not live in a fucking world where both my girls don't exist! I place my phone in my pocket and pull out my gun. I take one breath before I boot the door open and rush in. I scan side to side, checking the kitchen while Bishop and the twins, followed by Gage, Mav, Luka and a couple other guys, rush in. I take off toward Allison's room with my stomach bottoming out on the way.

"Amelia!" I scream.

"Daddy!" I hear her cry. I bought Allison a bed on gas struts so she can store shit beneath it. I grip the handle and lift it, tears springing to my eyes as I drop to my knees and open my arms. Mela drops Allison's phone and leaps into my arms sobbing. I hear my brothers sigh behind me in relief. I push her back and scan her from head to toe for any injuries.

"Are you hurt?" She shakes her head. "Can you tell Daddy what happened?" Her bottom lip wobbles and the tears flow faster. Knight drops down beside me and smiles like nothing is wrong, then reaches out to tuck her hair behind her ear. Her face is stained from her tears, her nose is red.

"Meelz, just tell your old man quickly what happened and me and uncle Cook will take you for ice cream and soda. But you got to promise you can't tell your mom when your dad brings her back." I stare at my brother in awe. He and Rook have been encouraging Mela to call Allison mom. She has slowly started to do it but has never said it to Allison directly... tonight is the first she has ever said it to me.

"I want my mommy," she cries. Knight pulls her from me and I growl. He holds my stare as he wraps his arms around Mela.

"Trust me, brother." I search his gaze for a second, then turn to Bishop who nods his head encouraging me to agree, so I nod. "Can you guys give us a minute." I open my mouth to tell him to fuck off but he pushes on. "She'll open up if she thinks it's our secret. She thinks she's in trouble with you and Allison, King. Trust me, brother, and I swear to you, we will get *your* girl back." I reach out, grip the back of his neck and yank him forward. I rest my head against his.

"Find her, please. I can't lose her, Knight!"

"I will, brother." I stand and leave. Walking away from my daughter when she needs me the most is the hardest thing I have ever fucking done but I need to trust Knight. I stop in the living room when I see Gage squatting down and looking at the floor. Luka and Mav stand around him.

"What is it?" Gage slowly rises to his feet, the guilt in his gaze pisses me off. "Answer me!" I yell, he doesn't flinch or recoil just nods and steps aside. I feel bile rise up my throat. Right there, next to the couch, are Allison's panties. That's not the worst part. Next to them is a small pool of blood. I drop to my knees and yank on my hair screaming... I should have fucking been here! They fucking took her to get to me. They wanted to hurt me so they went after my heart. They will all fucking die for ever thinking they could touch what was mine and get away with it. I give myself another minute before I slowly climb to my feet, lock down all my emotions and channel my inner beast. I'll let him out to play for as long as he needs to bring Allison back. Gage nods in a show of respect. Luka steps forward and places a hand on my shoulder.

"I'll head back to base and track all the cameras and get a plate to trace. We'll get her back." I nod unable to even speak.

"Mav, round the men up. I want a dozen guards at the house around the clock."

"Yes, boss."

"Find out where Michael is with Kiara. I want her inside and not in the pool house. We're at war now, you make sure that fucking house is locked down tight. My fiancée and niece will be there, anything happens to them and I'm coming for you." Mav nods, pulls out his phone and leaves. Bishop moves to stand next to Gage. His eyes are vacant and I can tell he has gone into beast mode like me.

"What do you want me to do?" Bishop slowly turns to Gage.

"Get back to the house, stay with Kiara." Her grips the front of Gage's shirt and hauls him in close. "You fucking protect her and Mela." Gage doesn't hesitate to agree.

"I swear to you, no harm will come to either of them, Bish." He releases Gage and nods just as Knight walks in. I look for Rook and Mela but he shakes his head.

"I told her to wait with Rook. She's fucking terrified, King." I scrub a hand down my face and curse. "She'll get through this." I nod.

"What did she say?" Knight darts his gaze away, his hands clench into fists at his side and my panic rises inside me. "Just fucking say it." I hate that I sound broken.

"She said Allison told her to hide and stay quiet until... she couldn't hear her scream anymore." I keep my emotions in check even though I want to paint the streets red with the blood of those that wronged me. "Then she told her to call you and tell you to come to her and that Daddy would... look after her. She also told Mela to tell you that she... loves you." I can't handle this shit. I push past Knight, run to the bedroom and grab Mela from Rook. No one questions me as I snag her teddy from the couch and walk out the fucking door. Chaos is waring inside me, the thirst for the blood of my enemies runs through my veins. I'm the underboss for a reason. I do all the gruesome things that Bishop can't. I'm the one who makes grown ass men squeal like pigs and squeal they shall when I find them!

Two weeks...

I wipe the blood from my hands on an old rag as his moans and pleas fall on deaf ears. It's been a long time since I was able to fully let myself go and actually enjoy the misery of my victims. I look to the side to find Bishop and Gage standing in the doorway. Bish may be able to fool others into thinking he is unaffected but I can see it in his eyes that the sight of Marco Valleo has him squeamish.

"Jesus," Gage breaths out, his disgust just fuels my need for more blood. I slowly turn away from the table that holds all the tools I need and admire my handy work. Marco's head is lulled to the side, on the verge of passing out again. One hand is fingerless, the other has bamboo spikes shoved under his nails. Nails stick out of his torso, his kneecaps are shattered.

"I don't know where she is," he cries out. I grab the needle from my pocket and shove it into his chest.

"What was that?" I smirk as I turn to Gage.

"Shot of adrenaline. Can't have him passing out now and missing the best part of the show." Gage shudders at my answer but Bishop remains unaffected. I turn back to Marco and grip his hair until he is looking up at me.

"I want to know where Romello is keeping her. Tell me what I want to know and I'll end it quickly." Marco isn't a loyal foot solider, he would sell you to anyone who pays the right price.

"I swear, I don't know." I grab the pliers from my pocket and he begins to thrash against his restraints. It's futile, he will never be able to break free. I slowly lift them to his mouth and he tries to clamp it closed.

"Open or I'll break your jaw." I can see him trying to figure out his next move but he doesn't have one.

"Romello is acting alone!" I pause and slowly lower the pliers as I take a step back.

"Tell me more. If you lie to me, I'll drag this out for weeks!" He nods his head and I can tell from how sluggish it is he doesn't have weeks, hours maybe.

"The money stopped coming in and he lost it. Donny..." He's Romello's underboss and a sick son of a bitch at that. "... and him went to the other families and tried to get them to take you all out."

"Why?" Bishop asks, his voice is calm but I know inside he is raging.

"Because you took Tony out." Bishop cocks his head to the side acting confused. No one outside of my *family* knows that Bishop was the one to end Tony. What Bish did can't go unpunished, it is our deepest secret.

"Did I?" Marco eyes Bishop for a beat and I can see that now he isn't sure.

"Well... That's what was said. The others aren't happy with you taking over. Mike and Donny went to Pauly and Vinny and they came up with a... plan." His eyes slowly droop so I reach out and smack him. He snaps his eyes open and shakes his head as best he can.

"Get on with it," I snap.

"They... are... to Russians." I don't need to hear more. I pull my gun and shoot him right in the middle of his head.

"What the fuck?" I turn to Gage and point my gun at him. Bishop eyes me, warning me not to kill my half-brother.

"Don't ever fucking question me. They are working with the Russian scum to get the skin trade back up and running. He didn't know where Allison was, so he is of no use to me." Bishop steps in front of Gage and I slowly lower my gun to my side.

"I've let you have your fun for a couple weeks, now it is time for you to reign in your rage and think like a boss." I sneer at him.

"I'm not the fucking boss, you are! This is what I do, Bishop," I shout as I wave my arms around the grungy darkened room. This is where I conduct my business, my own torture chamber!

"No, you are hiding out here so you don't have to face your fucking kid! She needs you, King, not me, or the twins or even fucking Gage and Kiara. Tend to your daughter and fix shit with her, then you will be able to fucking focus." He turns to leave but pauses in the doorway and peers back over his shoulder. "And for fuck's sake, take a goddam shower and eat something. I don't want to see another drop of whiskey near you!" I glare at the fucker. He may be the boss but he doesn't fucking tell me how to live my life.

Chapter Sixteen

Allison

I'm so cold.

I sit shivering in the corner of the room, my arms wrapped around my naked body. My head rests on the tops of my knees. I've stopped crying, there is no point in shedding tears when all they do is make them happy to know they are affecting me. I think about her every day and hope to God that she did as I asked and called King. I have never been more grateful for being able to shut off emotions and act on instinct, until that night. I just passed by the window and saw three blacked out SUV's skid to a stop outside my building, I knew they were there for me. I got Mela and put her under my bed. I will never be able to erase the fearful look in her eyes from my memory for as long as I live. I told her to hide, stay quiet and not make a sound. Not to come out or call King until I stopped screaming. I knew they would make me scream.

They beat me.

They cut my panties from my body and made sure to dig the knife in deep enough to draw blood, they wanted King to know they had hurt me. They tried to beat Mela's whereabouts out of me but I would rather burn in hell than ever let these sorry excuses for humans near my girl. Their leader, Mikey they call him, isn't the one that terrifies me. It's his underboss—Donny. That man has no semblance of humanity inside his body. I know I called King and his family monsters but they aren't. They love and care but Donny doesn't. He just wants to maim and hurt. He aims to inflict as much pain as he can every time he comes to see me. I have been beaten, starved and defiled in the worst fucking way. They may use my body and try to break me but I shut off, allowing my mind to wonder to a happy place to escape the torture they inflict on me.

I picture King, Mela and I all together, living as a family, happy and content. I think of Mela going to school with King and I dropping her off on her first day. The twins, Bishop, Kiara and Gage all standing around as they wave off our girl. That's my happy place. I have no family. My parents cut me off when I begged Christine to keep Mela. I was never the favorite child, just the mistake that came after the golden kid. I grew up knowing I was never loved. I think that's why I make sure to tell Mela daily how much I love her and even without words I want her to feel the love I have for her radiating off of me. The sound of the lock clicking has me tensing. I keep my eyes closed and just wait. I don't fight anymore, there isn't a point as they enjoy it more when I fight them off. I have lost count of the number of men that have come and had their *turn* as they call it.

They don't use condoms and it scares me more to think that I could become pregnant from one of these bastards. The door opens and I wait for them to grab me and throw me down on the disgusting mattress and rape me.

"Get the fuck in there!" I keep still but blink my eyes open and stifle my gasp when I see them push another girl into the room. She falls to her knees and cries out. I flinch, she needs to shut up or they will beat her for making a sound. The only time they allow you to wail or scream is when they are fucking you, other than that they beat you for making a noise. Shit, you don't even need to make a sound for them to come and blow off steam by hurting you. The door slams shut. The girl jumps to her feet and spins around banging on the door. I watch as she tries to find the handle... she won't find one, the door can only be opened from the other side.

"Let me out!" she screams. I shrink further back into the corner, praying for her to shut the fuck up!

"Be quiet," I hiss. She screams in fright and stumbles back a step, then looks around the room until she lands on my shadowy figure in the corner, hiding like a coward.

"Who's there?"

"Keep your voice down!" I scold. She moves toward me slowly. The closer she gets, the more tense I become. My muscles scream in protest, every part of my body aches and screams from the smallest movement. She crouches down in front of me and that's when I notice she isn't naked like me, she is fully clothed.

"Who are you?" she whispers. I open my mouth to answer but quickly clamp it closed. If I have learned one thing from being here it's that you can't trust anyone. For all I know, she could be working for Mike or Donny and here to set me up.

"No one," I mutter. She scoffs.

"If you found yourself here, in this place, then you clearly are someone and you must be important or at least important to *someone*." I eye her skeptically. For a woman who has just been thrown into a room that reeks of shit and piss, she doesn't seem affected or scared at all. I run my gaze over her using the only light from the barred window on the side of the room. The moon isn't as bright tonight so lighting isn't the best in here, just how I like it... then I can't see their faces.

"Why are *you* here?" She blows out a breath and runs her hand through her long straight blonde hair. It's so long I can see it nearly touches the ground from her crouched position.

"I was born into the wrong family," she whispers the words more to herself. Her disdain is clear from the tone of her voice. She doesn't have tanned skin so I know she isn't Italian. Who is this girl? "What's your name?"

"Allison." It feels weird to talk, my voice sounds hoarse from lack of use.

"Well, Allison, I'm Koby. The way I see it, we are each other's only hope of getting the fuck out of here!" I wish I shared her enthusiasm but I don't, it's been weeks and still no one has come to my rescue. I don't blame them though. I know King would be looking after Mela and that's all that matters. Don't get me wrong, I know King cares about me but maybe just not as much as I thought.

Days have passed and still I am bound to this shithole of a room, though ever since Koby arrived they haven't come for me. I'm so grateful for the reprieve and my body is slowly recovering from their beatings. I don't let my guard down though. I know they will be back, men like Donny don't just leave their toys alone, they kill them so there are no loose ends. As if my imagination conjured them the lock clicks and the door opens. Koby is on her feet and raising her fists ready to fight, the sight shocks me. It's daylight and I hate when they come during the day, I slink into the shadows and hide, not that it works, but the darkness does help to mask their faces when they are on top of me. The man steps into the room and doesn't even bat an eye at Koby. He swings his soulless eyes to me and flicks his head toward the bed. Normally I would obey and save myself the beating but... I can't. I don't want Koby to see they have beaten me into submission. I don't want her to know that I have given up and allow them to do whatever the fuck they want with my body.

His lip pulls back in a sneer as he kicks the door closed and storms over to me. I shrink into the corner of the room and cry out when he grips my hair and yanks me forward. I don't have time to process anything before his fist connects with my jaw and pain flares to life inside me. He uses his grip on my hair to hurl me onto the mattress. I roll to my side and curl up in a fetal position. He kicks me in the back, making me scream out in pain. Another blow lands, this time my ribs. My vision turns hazy from the pain. He slumps down on top of me, then uses his knees to kick my legs open. I try to push him off but he grips my hands in one of his and slaps me with the other before spitting in my face. It drips down my cheek as tears spring to the surface.

"You stupid cunt. Now I'm going to fucking rip your ass open and you're going to take it like the dirty slut you are!" I close my eyes as he flips me onto my stomach. At the sound of his belt buckle jiggling, I retreat inside my mind and try to go to my happy place. I feel the tip of his cock against my ass cheek and try to tense, but it only makes it more painful when I tense up. He parts my cheeks and spits. I feel his saliva drip down my crack and then he rubs it over my hole. I can't get to my happy place! A whimper escapes me as I feel the head of his cock press against my hole and wait for him to slam inside me.

"Fuck this," I hear Koby mutter before the guy grunts behind me, then the weight of his body is gone. I roll over and watch as Koby stomps on his hard dick. He shouts out in pain before she kicks him right in the mouth with her combat boot. She reaches down and pulls his knife from its sheath and plunges it right into his throat. I'm stunned and watch as he chokes on his own blood.

"Sdokhni gryaznaya svin'ya." (*Die you filthy, pig.*) I gasp as I dart my eyes to Koby. She's Russian! "Ty ponyatiya ne imeyesh', s kem ty trakhalsya." (*You have no idea who you fucked with.*) Koby turns to look down at me. I can never seem to get a read on her, she is as closed off emotionally as Knight. Her green eyes bore into mine as she gathers her long hair and ties it into a high ponytail. "Don't fucking look at me like that." Her harsh words snap me from my stupor.

"You don't have an accent but... you're Russian?" Her eyes harden.

"I told you I was born into the wrong family. Now, unless you want to get out of here stark fucking naked help me get his shirt off. Others will come looking for him soon." I can't move. As I stare at her, she drops down and begins to pull his shirt up. "Fucking move!" I jump into action and help her pull his shirt off. It's covered in blood but it beats being naked. The feeling of having clothes on again is strange. It makes me feel like I have a shield around my body, like a knight's armor. Koby turns to me and for the first time since she arrived, I see a look in her eyes I recognize... mistrust. She lifts a gun that I didn't even see she grabbed from the foot solider and points it at me. "Who are you really, Allison?" I raise my hands and open and shut my mouth like a gaping fish. "Answer me now or I'll shoot you where you stand!"

"I'm Allison Vaughn, I'm twenty-one years old—"

"Not that!" I stare at her unsure what I'm supposed to have said.

"Why are you here? Which family do you belong to?" I gulp before standing tall, if I'm going to die here, I am not going out easily.

"Who the fuck are you, Koby? No one has come in here since the day you arrived. They used to come like clockwork but not since you were thrown in here. Why the fuck should I tell you—"

"Because I am the only chance you have of getting the fuck out of here and back to your daughter." I stumble back a step.

"How do you know about her?" Fear grips me at the thought of her knowing about Mela, we may have made small talk but we never disclosed our private life whilst being locked in here together.

"I know about all of them and you." I grit my teeth.

"Then why fucking ask?" I snap. She slowly lowers the gun and tucks it into the back of her cargo pants.

"Because, you had a gun to your head and you never name dropped. You could have threatened me with your affiliation to the Murdoch's, but you didn't." This girl is fucking confusing. "I need to know one thing?"

"What?" I eye her skeptically.

"Can you guarantee me protection through the family if

I get you out of here?" I open my mouth but close it. I don't know how to answer that.

"I don't know, you saving me from... that," I motion to the body that lay between us, "will go a long way with them but... I don't even know who you are." She takes a deep breath and stands tall. She is taller than me so I have to look up.

"A friend, Allison. I'm a friend who can get you the fuck out of here alive and back to your family."

"I can't promise you anything, but I can promise that I will fight for you." She nods.

"I respect that."

Chapter Seventeen

Allison

The day passes at a snail's pace, I've been on edge waiting for them to come looking for their fallen guard all day. Night has fallen and Koby doesn't even seem bothered by the prospect of them coming for us. My jaw still aches and my ribs are burning but I block out the pain as I wait for whatever is to come next. I know they will come searching soon, there is no way this fugly piece of shit's disappearance hasn't gone unnoticed. I don't know why I never thought to disarm them or use their own weapons against them. The sounds of shouting outside the door has me on my feet. Koby stands beside me and hands me the knife. I stare at it for a moment before shaking my head, she sighs and grips my hand placing the knife in my palm. I try to yank free of her touch. She stares down at me for a moment before understanding flickers through her gaze.

"It will fade but it will never go away. You will get used to the touch of others again over time. They come at you, use the pointy end to stab them and you don't stop. Don't scream like movies show you do. Be silent and remain calm or they will alert everyone and we will never get out." I try to muster the courage I will need to do as she asks, then she grabs my arm and drags me after her. We flatten ourselves against the wall behind where the door will open. I try to quieten my breaths, feeling my heart thumping against my ribs. Gun shots ring out outside and I bite my lip to stop the scream from tearing out of me. The door swings open and a man walks in. Before I can even comprehend what is about to happen, Koby lifts her gun and fires a single shot into the back of the guy's head without batting an eye. She swivels around and darts out the door before rushing back in and grabbing the weapons from the *second* dead guy. She comes to me and grabs the knife, replacing it with a gun. "You point and pull the trigger. The safety is off. Don't fucking hesitate or you will die!" I block out all my fear and nod. She grips my hand in hers and pulls me after her. We stay against the walls. Every corner we come to she stops and peers either side before we're running again.

We round another corner and stop at the bottom of a set of stairs, we must be in the basement of a building. She holds her gun in front of her, so I do the same. Just as I get my foot on the first step, Koby swings around and shoots. I look back with my heart in my throat as a guy crumples to the ground. I stare up at her shock, but she doesn't falter as she continues up the stairs and I follow after her. We encounter three more men on our way that Koby drops without thought. Once we reach the top, shouts and shots can be heard all around. Koby raises her gun as a group of men run past but I push the gun down, something big is happening, these men aren't out looking for us.

"What the fuck are you doing?" she hisses.

"You shoot and they will all be focusing on us. Something is happening outside. We can use their distraction to slip out the back." Her eyes search mine for a moment before she nods stiffly and grips my hand, then we are off running in the opposite direction the men came from. More foot soldiers pass us, shooting us curious glances but say nothing. My heart is beating so fast and my hands are clammy, I must look like roadkill but still, no one stops us. We come to a halt at a door with a small glass window. Koby curses before stunning me.

"Stay here!" I grab her arm and hold her in place as fear grips me.

"Where are you going?"

"I may be able to kill but I can't hotwire a fucking car. I saw a desk with keys on it back there. Wait here for me and I'll be back." She yanks her arm free before I can protest. I slink back into the shadow of the room and pray no one comes in. I hold the gun in front of me, calm my breathing and push my rising panic down at the thought of Koby not coming back and leaving me here. I have a new sense of renewed worth. That room took my fight from me and I vow here and now to never let that happen again. I will fight for my life and fight to get back to my... *daughter*. Just the thought of her has determination thrumming through me. I hear voices and keep my eyes on the door, lift my gun and hold it steady.

Don't hesitate!

Koby's word play on repeat in my mind, two men enter the room and the first one's eyes widen at the sight of me. I don't think, but pull the trigger and gasp. He reels back and grunts as he grips his shoulder. I shoot again and this time it hits him in the stomach making him drop to his knees. I'm too focused on the first guy to even see the second one tackle me from the side. I land on the ground with a grunt, the gun slipping from my hands. He rolls me onto my back and uses his weight against me. He wraps his hands around my neck and I thrash beneath him, clawing at his arms. I gasp but can't draw a breath. I punch his chest but he doesn't budge. I spot the hilt of his knife strapped to his waist as my vision is turning hazy. I grip the knife and don't even hesitate as I draw my arm back and stab him in the chest. His eyes widen and he drops to the side. I crawl away from him and grab the gun, then stand, gasping for air. He climbs to his feet with pain etched on his face. He comes for me and I shoot, hitting him right in the side of the throat. Blood sprays out and coats the side of my face as I turn away. He drops to the floor with a heavy thud and I just stand here staring down at him in a numb state.

"Good work." I blink up at Koby who seems proud of what I just did. I don't ponder that as she throws the door open with her gun pointed in front of her. I follow after her and do the same, she clicks a set of keys and a jeep beeps, we both take off toward the green jeep. I throw the passenger door open and dive in. She shoves the keys in the ignition and turns them. The car roars to life. She slams it into drive and plants her foot. I notice as we drive away that we're at the docks. The building I was being held in is one of the main offices here. I need to recall every detail I can of this place so when I see King again, I can tell him to burn this fucking place down!

Chapter Eighteen

King

I'm back in my torture shack. I've come to love this place over the past few weeks. It's been nearly five weeks since Allison has been gone. We raided the docks three weeks ago when we got a tip off that a shipment was being sent out of girls, searched the whole fucking place and couldn't find Allison anywhere! I turn back to my two comrades and smile wide, each of them has a ball gag in their mouths, I haven't done anything hasty, I want to drag out their pain make these cunts suffer for touching her. I run my gaze over Mike Romello, the fat piece of shit pissed himself within two minutes of being strapped to that chair. I look back to Donny, he is harder to crack. He doesn't scream out for mercy or even beg for me to stop. I run the tip of my Swiss blade along the top of Mike's thigh. he shakes like a leaf and I chuckle.

"You are the Don of your family, yet you sit here in your own piss and shit." He tries to mutter something but I can't make out what it is thanks to the gag. All his men are gone, the ones who he named that touched Allison were slaughtered like the pigs they were. They didn't fucking suffer enough if you ask me. Thirteen different men touched my girl and I hate myself even more for bringing her into my world. She is my queen and she fucking overturned me the moment she stepped into my life. I planned to torment her, punish her for her crimes against me but the truth is, she had me in check from the moment I met her at the diner. Her big blue eyes held me captive; her sinful lips trapped me in a trance I still haven't woken from. I unclasp his gag and he gags a couple times before dragging in lungfuls of air. The sight of this fat piece of shit disgusts me.

"I don't know where she is. She was in the basement like I told you! You can't kill me, boy, I am the head of the Romello—" The door swings open and I turn to see Bishop. The look in his eyes has me on edge. I shove the gag back into Mike's mouth before following Bishop out of the room. We climb the concrete steps out of the bunker in our backyard. The bunker is in the woods behind our house. When we reach the top, I nod to the two men who guard it.

"No one goes down there." They each nod and step back to close the heavy metal doors, to anyone who stumbled upon the bunker it just looks like a bomb shelter. I follow Bishop toward the house, an uneasy feeling stirring inside me. We enter the back door and I scan my head side to side to make sure Mela isn't around. I'm covered in blood and she doesn't need to see me like this. "Where's Mela?"

"Gage took her for Ice cream." I nod, the twins and

Kiara have been studying from home as Bishop won't allow them to leave the estate until we have dealt with this situation. I hate that he refers to Allison being gone as a fucking *situation*... she is so much more than that! I follow Bishop into his office and drop down into one of the chairs in front of his desk. Luka and Mav stroll in a second later. I lean back and close my eyes for a second, exhaustion thrums through me. I haven't slept much these past few weeks. I lay with Mela every night until she sleeps and I just lay beside her and stare. She hasn't been happy or smiled much since Allison has been gone. I never noticed it before but I do now. I was so fucking wrong the day I told Allison she wasn't Mela's mother. She didn't need to give her life to carry that title. Mela isn't whole without her here and I will do anything and everything I need to bring the mother of my daughter back to her—back to me, where she belongs! "Show him." I sit up in my chair as Luka passes me a laptop. I flick my gaze to him in question.

"Press play," is all Luka says before he steps back. I push play and watch the grainy camera footage. My breath halts in my lungs, my eyes zero in on my girl. She looks thin and... different. I can't explain it. Her eyes don't hold that look of pure untainted innocence anymore. I spot the leggy blonde behind her and narrow my eyes. She places a hand on Allison's back and ushers her out of the building as the video cuts out.

"Who the fuck is that bitch?" I growl.

"We don't know. We have run her face through all our software and nothing comes up." I ignore Luka as I focus on Bishop.

"How long have you had this tape?" He doesn't seem put out by my angry tone.

"Two days." I stand and the laptop tumbles to the floor as I glare down at my brother.

"And you didn't think to fucking tell me you had found her?" I yell.

"I was waiting until I had a lead and—"

"And fucking what, Bishop?"

"I have one." That has me clamping my mouth shut. "She's in the city but she isn't alone."

"Who else aside from the blonde is with her?" I grit out.

"A Russian." *No, Allison would never sell us out like that, would she?*

"Where is she, Bishop and don't fucking lie to me." He shoots a look to Luka and nods for him to take over.

"She's at the Four Seasons in the penthouse." I close my eyes and breath in through my nose. I know this looks bad but I just know she isn't a plant, she can't be.

"King?" I don't even look at Bishop as I answer.

"I know," I say barely above a whisper.

"I can... do it." I shake my head, I appreciate the fact he would carry this burden for me but it isn't his burden to bear, it's mine.

"No, if she is a plant then I want to be the one to look her in the eye as I pull the trigger." My voice is hollow and devoid of emotion.

"King?" I slowly flick my gaze to Bishop's making sure to keep my mask in place. He can never know that the thought of killing Allison is killing *me* inside.

"What?"

"If she is a plant, then I need the three of them alive. I'll need information... extracted." I nod.

"Understood." I can feel Mav and Luka's stare burning into the side of my head. I know what Bishop is asking me to do and I'll do whatever I have to ensure the safety of my family and my daughter, even if that means torturing the woman I love.

Three days...

I've been scoping out their routes, what they do, trying to distinguish a habit or some form of routine. I haven't seen them leave the hotel once which tells me they are either disguising themselves or they are still holed up in the penthouse. I pull my phone out and dial Gage's number. I hate to admit it but I have come to respect the bastard. He has proven himself loyal to the family and has even earned my trust enough to take Mela out without me wanting to kill him. One of our men bumped into Mela outside and Gage nearly shot him for knocking her down and making her shed a tear. From that day on he has been known as *Uncle* Gage.

"What's up, King?"

"Where is she?"

"We're about to light a fire out back, the twins and Kiara want to do smores." I nod even though he can't see me. "She's asking for you."

"Put her on."

"Yeah, but just one thing."

"What is it , Gage, you want money?" He growls.

"I don't need your fucking money, asshole."

"Then what do you want?"

"If shit goes south and you need to *bring her* in, I can do it for you." That has me pausing, I didn't expect him to offer that.

"If anyone is going to be exacting revenge on Allison, it will be me."

"Got it, here's Meelz," he says before handing the phone to her.

"Hi, Daddy." The sound of her voice alone has a smile spreading across my face.

"Hi, baby girl."

"I miss you." My heart skips a beat.

"I miss you too. Daddy will be home soon, okay?"

"Okay, but are you bringing Mommy home too?" I freeze, how the fuck do I answer that?

"Meelz, come on Uncle Cook wants you," I hear Gage say, the bastard has me on speaker phone. I smirk, well played brother, well played.

"Bye, Daddy. I love you."

"Bye, baby. I love you to." I wait a second before Gage speaks.

"She's gone."

"Speakerphone huh?" He chuckles.

"What can I say, I thought you might need saving and you did."

"Thank you." He's silent for a beat before he answers.

"Anytime, brother." I end the call and gaze up at the building, I'll wait a few more hours before I tear shit up and get answers from my girl. I pray to God she isn't a fucking plant because I don't know if I would be able to watch the life drain from her eyes.

Chapter Nineteen

Allison

I can feel eyes on me. I slowly roll over and freeze, a shadow stands in the corner of my room and I choke down my scream. I slowly sit up in bed and clutch the blanket to my chest, I've been plagued with nightmares every single night since Koby brought me here. I don't sleep. I may drift off but I wake only after a couple moments. My room is shrouded in darkness, the figure steps forward and a whimper escapes me—I knew we made it of there too easy. I knew they would come back to silence me! In a second the figure is on top of me with a hand clamped over my mouth muting my scream, tears fall on their accord. I thrash beneath the heavy weight of him on top of me, I won't go down without a fucking fight.

"You played me, baby." I still, everything inside me

freezes at the sound of his voice. I breath in through my nose and try to calm my nerves, he's here! "I'm gonna move my hand and if you scream, I'll put a bullet in your head without remorse, nod if you understand." I gulp as I nod. He moves off me and I scramble to sit up. I move to switch on the bedside lamp and I'm blinded for a moment. I blink a couple times before I focus on him. His hair is a mess as if he has been tugging at the strands, his eyes haunted, black circles evident beneath his eyes.

"King..." I breath, his eyes narrow and I clamp my mouth shut. His eyes scan over me taking in my yellowing bruises that cover my body. He rips the covers from my legs and I automatically tense. He runs his hands down my thighs and I fight the urge to pull my legs back, his thumbs skim over my battered and bruised flesh.

"What did they do to you?" he whispers so low I can barely make the words out. I don't bother answering. The bruises between my inner thighs are evidence enough of what I went through at the hands of his enemies.

"They didn't do shit!" I'm proud of how my voice doesn't waiver and I sound strong even though I feel anything but that. His gaze lazily flicks back to mine. He has his emotions shut down so I can't see what he is thinking.

"I'm gonna ask you this once... don't lie to me, Allison."

"Don't you dare come in here and make demands of me!" I snap.

"Or what? You'll scream for your Russian boyfriend to come save you?" My eyes widen in horror, he knows about Dimitri! "You played me so good, baby. Your pussy and good girl virgin act was something I never saw coming. You used my daughter to get inside my head. You used your charms to lull me into loving you... I fucking let you into my family and you betray me!" I flinch at the angry tone of his voice.

"You don't know anything!" He reaches out but I flinch away. A pained look enters his eyes and I hate that he can see the fear inside me, the fear *they* installed in me.

"Fuck!" He scrubs a hand down his face. "Allison, I don't want to hurt you!" The anguish is evident in his tone.

"Then don't," I plead.

"Are you working with the Russian's?" I bite my lip and watch as his gaze hardens.

"It's... complicated." He bares his teeth and I grimace.

"Uncomplicate it, Allison, I need to know now!"

"Why?" He jumps to his feet and begins to pace the length of my room.

"Because if you are, I have to... get the information from you the only way I know how." I gasp.

"You would rape me?" He stills and stares down at me in horror.

"What the fuck? I would never rape a woman!" he spits. "Why would you ask me..." He cuts himself off when I drop my gaze to my lap. He sits down beside me and grips both my hands in his. He reaches out slowly, giving me every chance to pull away. He grips my chin tenderly and lifts it until my gaze meets his. "Baby, are you working against my family? I need you to answer me that. If the answer is no, then please say it because I need to hold you." A strangle sob tears from me as I shake my head in answer. "Thank fuck," is all he says before he's grabbing and pulling me into his lap where I bury my face in the crook of his neck and weep. I cling to him like he can chase all the bad from within me. I hold him close hoping that he puts all the scattered pieces of my broken body back together again.

I feel myself retreating inside my head and this time I

don't know if I will be able to come back from the darkness that tries to consume me daily. My mind was my friend whilst I was in that room, but ever since I have been freed... it's become my worst enemy. It plays tricks on me and makes me think I'm being followed or I feel a ghost of touch over my body each night. I can feel it pulling me into the deepest recesses of my mind, waiting to consume and make me numb to the world and all the pain that I suffered.

"Her birthday is the thirtieth of May, 2018." His voice seems so far away, I want to latch onto it. "Her favorite color isn't just one, she loves purple and pink. Her favorite animal is a unicorn." The sound of his voice and hearing him talk about *her* has me wanting to fight my way out of the darkness, to come back to *them*. "Her name... her name is Amelia Queen... Murdoch. You gave my baby girl my last name and named her after me in your own quirky way. Come back to us, baby."

I want to come back to him, to come back to them both, but being present means I have to deal with the pain and nightmares that plague me all hours of the night. Even in the daylight, the monsters come from the shadows to try draw me to them. Koby and Dimitri have tried to help but knowing all those men are still out there and that they can get to me whenever they want has me shutting down, a piece of me has died each day.

I'm tired, I don't want to fight anymore. I want to give up.

Chapter Twenty

King

I sit here and watch as the will to live slowly drains from her eyes. I don't know why she is staying here with these Russian scum, but knowing that she isn't working with or for them means I don't have to kill her. I don't have to extract information from her. I just need to bring her back to me though, I can't take her home like this. Mela can't see her mother in this... state. I thought maybe telling her everything I have learned about our daughter would bring her back to me but I think I need to go down a darker path. I can see that darkness now taints her pure heart, my own darkness calls to hers.

"Thirteen. I executed all of them for ever thinking they could lay a finger on what is mine. I wanted to draw out their agony and relish in their screams for what they did to you." Her eyes slowly begin to focus as my words start to register in her mind. "I cut each of their cocks off and nailed it to their heads as each of them were executed... Two remain alive." For the first time since coming here I see something other than fear in her blue eyes, I see vengeance.

"Who?" She no longer sounds meek or unsure, her voice is firm and strong. I know her healing from the events she suffered through will take time for her to overcome, and I'll be by her side every step of the fucking way!

"Mike and Donny." She leaps from my hold and stares down at me. I search her face for any indication of what she is thinking but she has a mask of indifference in place.

"I want them." I stare up at her in confusion.

"What?" I need her to spell it out for me. I need to hear the words from her mouth before I allow my baby to go anywhere near these sick twisted fucks to exact her revenge.

"I want to *play* with them. I want to make them *bleed* and watch them writhe in agony and laugh at their pain as I inflict it upon their bodies." I can tell they have said something similar to her but the way she delivers her speech has my cock hard and wanting to be buried balls deep inside her. She may not say it out loud, and I honestly don't know if I could handle hearing all the details of what she went through, but I know what they did to her.

"Then let me take you to them." She nods and stalks into the bathroom closing the door behind her. I stare at it for a moment a bit stunned on what the fuck she is up to, but she comes out a minute later dressed in all black and has her shoulder length hair tied in a messy bun atop her head. The look in her eyes tells me she is not my innocent Ally anymore—she has been tainted by the bad in my world and I will spend the rest of our lives hating myself for allowing any part of my fucked-up world to touch her. I stand and grip her hand in mine as I lead her out of the room. She slams to a stop as we enter the living room. Luka, Knight and four of my guys stand around the Russian guy and the blonde bitch with guns pointed at their heads. Allison yanks her hand from mine and rushes over to them. As soon as she steps in front of Luka and Knight, they both lower their guns slightly but not all the way.

"You want to kill them? You have to go through me and we all know you won't." I love how confident she sounds. She knows for a fact I would never allow them to lay a finger on her, but I don't butt in. I let her handle this. She needs to feel in control and like she has the power. Right now? She really fucking does.

"Ally..." Knight breathes her name like he can't quite believe she is actually standing in front of him. He drops the gun to his side before reaching out to her with the other and hugging her. Her whole body is stiff and I can tell that his touch is scaring her but she won't say it. My hands clench at my side. Those fuckers are going to pay for this. I am going to eradicate each of their family lines and make sure the Romello name never rises again. Ally pulls back but smiles up at Knight before pinning Luka with a look. He looks to me but I shrug letting him know it's her show not mine.

"Drop the gun now or I'll shoot you." My brows raise, I know she has no idea how to shoot... Before I can finish my thought, she draws a gun from the back of her waistband that I didn't even know she was fucking carrying and points it at Luka. Knight stares at her in shock while the other four point their guns at my girl. I step forward.

"Point that fucking gun at her again and I'll kill each of you and your mothers!" They lower their guns immediately. Luka on the other hand keeps his gun pointed at the guy while looking at Allison.

"You've changed, Allison." I see it now, her body doesn't give away and betray her fear like before. Her eyes don't show you her thoughts or feelings, she's like... me. And I don't know if I'm happy about that or not.

"Put the gun down or I will shoot you, Luka." They stand there silently staring at each other for a moment, neither of them willing to budge. I watch as she slowly moves her finger over the trigger and I actually think she may shoot my boy!

"Dostatochno," (*Enough.*) the blonde says. Allison peers down at her from the corner of her eye.

"She's a fucking Russian, Ally!" Knight shouts. Her body may not quiver in fear but I can see in her eyes that Knight's angry tone has her scared. Out of all my brothers, Knight was the closest to her, so the fact that him raising his voice makes her scared tells me the damage inflicted on her is worse than I thought. She slowly looks back to him and shakes her head.

"She isn't who you think she is... neither is he. They helped me. They kept me alive and she stopped me from being..." She doesn't need to finish, everyone in this room knows exactly what she was about to say. She puts her gun back into her waistband before turning to her *friends*. She crouches down and pulls a... knife from her boot. She had a fucking knife as well? She cuts through the cable ties and helps them both their feet. The woman is tall, a leggy blonde who stands almost eye level with Knight. My brother sneers at her in disgust. The woman isn't bothered as she displays nothing on her face, her body doesn't even tense or react. I look to the guy next. He seems timid... reserved and frightened. He drops his chin to his chest causing his black hair to flop onto his forehead. Allison reaches out and places her hand on his shoulder. I narrow my eyes, she better not fucking feel anything for this fucker. "Dimitri, it's okay." She grips his hand in hers and then turns to me motioning for me to join her. I'd like to say I went to her because she asked but that's a lie. I want this fucker to see from the look in my eyes that if he touches my girl, I'll skin him alive. He slowly lifts his green eyes to mine. It floors me to see absolute fear in his gaze. I furrow my brow, he's just a... kid.

"How old are you?" I'm shocked it's the first question that comes out of my mouth. The blonde yanks him back and blocks my view—six guns are now pointed at her as she glares at me.

"He is not of your concern!" Allison moves to stand in front of me almost like she is protecting me. I want to scoff at the idea but the truth is, it makes me hot for my girl.

"You asked me to help you *both*. I'm standing here trying to do that, Koby. Trust me like I trusted you." Koby, that's the leggy blonde's name. Her and Allison stand here in a stare off for a tense moment before she nods and Allison sighs. "Lower the bloody guns, she isn't armed!" Allison snaps.

"How can you be so sure?" Knight snaps.

"Want to try search me, Playboy?" The threat in Koby's voice is clear. Knight glares at her.

"Enough!" All eyes turn to Allison, my girl is taking charge. "Koby, you and Dimitri need to pack your shit, we're leaving." Uh, what?

"Yeah, no. Those Russian fucks aren't coming home with us." Koby sneers at Knight but doesn't get a chance to reply, Allison swirls on Knight and pins him with a dirty look.

"You want intel on the Russian's?" She doesn't give him a chance to answer. "They are the key to helping your family take them down! Either they come with me or I'm staying right here and you can deal with King's meltdown." I snicker at that, I don't fucking meltdown, ever!

"I'm calling Bishop," Luka mutters before he turns and walks out.

***

Bishop took a lot more convincing than Luka had thought. He relented but Koby and Dimitri would have guards stationed on them at all times—they will not be able to roam freely or even take a shit without someone knowing. The car is shrouded in tense silence. Allison refused to sit up front with me and sits in the back with Koby and Dimitri. Knight is tense beside me and I can't blame him, it has me on edge having the enemy behind me. I just want to get home and get Allison alone. I'm nervous at the fact of Mela seeing her. Allison hasn't even asked me about her and that is unsettling me the most. Mela *was* her everything and it seems like now her priorities have... shifted.

We pull up to the front of the house and I turn in my seat to look at each of them. Dimitri has his gaze on his lap, Allison has his hand clasped in hers. Koby, she surprises me when I see her taking in her surroundings and documenting everything she sees. Something tells me there is more to this girl than meets the eye. She holds herself in a way that tells me she is used to being underestimated and will surprise you at every turn.

We pile out of the cars. I move toward Allison as she stands here and just stares up at the house. She shows no emotion. Dimitri clings to her arm like she is the thing grounding him. I need to find out who these people are and how they are linked to my girl. The front door opens and

Bishop steps out with Mav beside him. His eyes scan over us with a detached look until he stops on Allison. For the briefest of seconds his eyes soften and relief shines in his eyes before he quickly masks it. He looks to the two Russian's and his stare goes from unbothered to downright hostile. He says something to Mav before turning and marching back into the house. Mav indicates for us to follow him. I fight the eye roll, I know the drill. We take them into Bishop's office, scare them and make it known that we are not to be fucked with and that we'll kill them without losing sleep if they try to fuck us over.

Knight walks in and drops down in the chair in front of Bishop's desk. Bish has his gaze fixed on the two Russian's as we walk in. Mav and Luka lean against the wall as I stand beside Allison. The boy still clings to her and Koby stands on his other side. Bish shoots me a look and I know what he wants, I step away from Allison and move to stand beside Bishop behind his desk. We need to show these two that we are a united family and won't tolerate shit... that they are only in here, in this house, because of Allison. If she is wrong in her judgment about these two it's my head on the chopping block. I vouched for them because of her.

"Give me one good reason why I don't put a bullet in each of your heads, right now?"

"Because, she saved me from getting raped... again." Allison's voice doesn't waiver, she doesn't drop her eyes from Bishop. She stands tall and owns her words. Bishop doesn't show his surprise or remorse for what she has been through, he has enough respect for her to not even pity her.

"You think your opinion matters?"

"I thought it didn't, then look where we are standing now. My opinion must hold some weight." I fight to keep the smile from my face. Bishop leans back in his chair and stares at her. I know he can see the change in her as well.

"You think because you're with my brother—"

"No, this has nothing to do with King and I, but it has everything to do with the fact *I* am Amelia's mother."

Chapter Twenty-One

Allison

Pride shines in King's eyes. Knight peers over his shoulder and smirks but I don't take my eyes off Bishop. King may be ruthless but Bishop is the one that calls the shots. If I am to keep true to my word, I need him to agree to allow Koby and Dimitri to stay. We don't know each other well but Koby also doesn't pity me. I see it in the three Murdoch's brother's gazes that they are trying to hide their pity. I don't need their fucking pity, I need them to treat me like Koby does. She doesn't beat around the bush or look at me like I'll cry every minute of the day.

"Don't over estimate yourself, Allison." His tone is flat and unwavering. "You still haven't given me a reason as to why they should remain breathing." I feel King staring at me and I know if I meet his stare my hardened exterior will crumble. I turn to Koby but can see she isn't about to say a damn thing and is leaving it all to me to keep them alive.

"Koby can help with your... Russian problem." He leans forward and steeples his arms on his desk.

"What problem might that be?" His condescending tone grates on my fucking nerves.

"The problem of your territory being infiltrated and the last remaining two families working against you to take you down." Bishop shoots his gaze to Koby, keeping the surprise from his face at her revelation. I know there is *way* more to Koby and Dimitri than they have shared but I haven't pushed them for information and they haven't asked me either. Our trust is built on our shared experience. Koby could have easily left me behind but she didn't. A part of me feels like if she didn't want to be there, she wouldn't have been.

"I already knew that," he snaps.

"She saved my life, Bishop. You have no fucking idea what it was like. You want to shoot her, then shoot me as well," I rage, my anger is coursing through me.

"No!" King snaps but I ignore him and push on.

"I wouldn't be standing here in front of all of you if it wasn't for her—"

"We were coming for you. They would never have killed you!" I shake my head, Bishop doesn't get it!

"It wasn't them that were going to kill me," I say barely above a whisper.

"What do you mean?" The uncertainty in King's voice tells me already knows the answer but just wants me to say it aloud. I look at him as I deliver the blow that I know will rock him to his core.

"They stripped me bare, used me and broke me a part. I had nothing left."

"You had me and Mela!" he shouts.

"No, you and Mela had each other, King. I had myself and I lost my will to live. I didn't want to live another second of that torture. The day Koby got us out, she wanted to bring me here. I said... no." The distraught look on his face crushes me but he needs to understand. "I couldn't allow you or Mela to see me..." Tears begin to prick the backs of my eyes but I will them back down. "I wanted to end my suffering. I wanted the pain to stop and I knew if you saw me you would try to take on that burden and I couldn't have that. I needed you to stay focused on Amelia and not be... brought down by my fucked-up state." He comes charging toward me and I tense in anticipation. Koby darts in front of me at the last second and I love her for it but King will kill her if she tries to keep me from him.

"You will not hurt her." The protectiveness in her tone has my heart swelling. Dimitri clings to my arm in fear. He has become so attached to me in the short amount of time I have known them.

"You ever and I mean ever try to keep her from me again and I'll make your worst nightmares seem like a daydream." I reach out and tap her on the shoulder letting her know it's okay and to step aside. She grunts out her disapproval but does as I ask. King strikes out so fast I don't even have time to prepare. I stifle my gasp when he grips my face and peers into my eyes.

"There will never be a lifetime where I don't find you. I will be the glue that keeps you together each time you feel like you're falling apart. Mela needs you, Allison... I fucking need you. Don't ever for a second think you are not worthy of living because, baby, you are the reason my life is worth anything. I love our daughter more than anything but I also love you so much it fucking hurts. I won't lose you, Allison, I can't." Tears flow freely down my cheeks at his endearing words of love.

"Y-you still want me even after what I just told you? I'm not a sweet little virgin anymore, King. I'm tainted fucking goods—" He growls right in my face.

"You aren't fucking tainted. You think you belong in the dark but baby let me tell you something, I am the fucking shadows that shroud you in the darkness. I'll be your shadow or your goddamn light... Fuck, I'll be whatever you need me to be." I hear the truth ring out in his words and my heart explodes. I want to latch onto him and allow him to make me forget but he can't. He cannot wipe away what happened to me. How can I love and hate him at the same time? I waited for him to find me and rescue me from the hell I was living in for weeks, in the end, I figured out I didn't need a fucking king to save me. I rose up like the fucking queen that *I* am and rescued myself.

"I can't..." He gives me a little shake and I clamp my mouth closed.

"You can and you will. You are not going to push me away. You want to yell, scream, hit me, fuck, do you want to shoot me?" I gasp.

"You'd let me shoot you?"

"No!"

"Yes," Bishop and King both answer in unison.

"You are not shooting my idiot brother, that is a fucking order, King." I can see it in his green eyes, if it's what I wanted he would disobey his Don's order and allow me to shoot him. I'm angry at him but I also don't want to mar his beautiful skin with a bullet hole either, but there is another option.

"I want a fight." King drops his hold and steps back. I spy Koby fighting her smile.

"The fuck?" I hold his stare as *I* shake off Dimitri and step into King.

"You heard me. You want me to hit you but I won't do it unless you fight back." He shakes his head.

"You can't fight, baby—" I scoff, of course he would still think that.

"Says who?" He shrugs.

"Me."

"Of course, you would think I'm some damsel in distress still. I didn't need you to fight my way out and kill off the guards. I did that. I also didn't need you to train me day and night to give me something else to focus on."

"Who the fuck taught you to fight?" Of course, that is all he would take from what I just said.

"I did," Koby answers for me. She doesn't show emotion often, she's like a statue but right now, pride shines in her eyes. King swings his gaze to her and if looks could burn you alive Koby would be ablaze right now.

"You taught my girl to fight?" His tone is flat and deadly, most people would cower but not Koby.

"I did. She was weak and easy prey but now, she will at least be able to put up a fight. If she continues her training there will be no way they will ever touch her... again." King grimaces at the reminder but says nothing as he turns and reclaims his place next to Bishop.

"They stay but not in the house, they can take up residence in the guest house." Of course, they have a guest house *and* a pool house. Fucking rich people! "You will have round the clock guards. If I so much as suspect you are plotting or if you try anything that makes me think you are up to something, you will be dead before you can blink."

"You both gonna be, okay?" I ask Koby and Dimitri as I stare at the guest house that is triple the size of my old apartment. King and Knight stand in the entryway. I want to stay with them but I also know King won't allow it. I also need to get over my fear and go see Mela.

"We'll be fine. You should go." Koby comes off as blunt and rude but after getting to know her these past couple of weeks, I've learned she just isn't someone who minces words. I nod and turn to leave but Dimitri grips my hand. King and Knight both move forward but I shake my head to them as I turn back to D. He is just a kid. He shouldn't have the amount of fear he does in his eyes. He is haunted by the life he has had to live. Koby is doing everything she can for him and I admire her for that.

"You stay?"

"I'm sorry D, I can't—" Koby cuts me off.

"Ostavte eye, ona dolzna uiti." (*Leave her, she must go.*) Dimitri nods and releases my hand. I feel bad for not being able to remain with him but I need to see my daughter and try work out what the hell I am going to do next... and whether or not King will be a part of my next step.

"I'll come back and see you tomorrow, okay?" Dimitri smiles but it doesn't reach his eyes.

"Go, he will be fine." I nod to Koby before turning to leave. Knight has his gazed fixed on the Russian beauty behind me. I stop in front of him and ignore King's heated gaze on me, I can't deal with him looking at me like that.

"Knight?" He slowly flicks his gaze down to me but I can see he is taut with tension. I love Knight but not even I know how deep the damage my sister caused runs through him. It breaks my heart to know my sister could have preyed on a fucking child and destroyed his innocence. I hate Christine for doing that to Knight!

"I'm staying," is all he says. I know this boy well enough to know that from the tone of his voice I won't be able to change his mind, so I just nod and follow King out without a backward glance.

Chapter Twenty-Two

King

She follows behind me silently, I can feel her eyes boring into the back of me but ignore it. I know she has been through a fucking lot, but I also will not pity her and handle her like a child. She doesn't need me treating her differently or covering her in bubble wrap. She needs me to give her something to use as an outlet. That's when the idea begins to form in my mind. I know what I have to do in order to not only help Allison heal and deal with her trauma, but it will also help Kiara. I just need Bishop to get on board with this or I'll be going against my Don and doing it anyway. I've never ignored an order from him but Allison needs this. My girl needs me to put her first and take into consideration her feelings and wants, and that is what I am going to do. We round the corner and head down the hall to my room but she pauses in front of Mela's room—her door is slightly ajar.

"Did she ask about me?" Her softly spoken words hold so much hurt.

"Every second of every day."

"What did you tell her?"

"That the bad men Daddy was away fighting found out he had two weaknesses. That because Mommy was so brave, they only took one instead of two of you." A strangled sob escapes her. I dart forward to take her into my arms but she moves forward and enters Mela's room. Not wanting to wake Mela I stand in the doorway and watch as Allison creeps over to her bed and stares down at our little girl. I cross my arms over my chest and lean against the door. Ally runs her fingers through Mela's hair and smiles even though tears leak from her eyes.

"I'm sorry I wasn't strong enough to save us both." My breath stills inside me. She places a tender kiss to Amelia's head before marching out of the room and down the hall to mine. I pull the door closed quietly and hustle after Allison. I storm into my room and find her at the foot of the bed staring at the mess of sheets and pillows on my bed.

"I didn't have time to clean up," I mutter as I brush past her to try and make the bed.

"You mean hide the evidence of your whores being over?" I drop the pillow and gawk at her, has she lost her fucking mind?

"You want to repeat that?" I growl in anger. She tries to look unaffected but the hurt in her eyes betrays her.

"How many whores did you have in here?" Anger thrums through me—how could she fucking think that?

"Unless you are referring to our daughter as a *whore*, then none. Only she has been in here with me." She flinches but I don't give a fuck. How could she think I would do that to her? "What do you want me to say, Allison?"

"Nothing." I can tell from the anger in her gaze she is pissed at me.

"Then why are you trying to pick a fight with me? Nothing I say is going to change what happened. I'm here trying to make it right, baby—"

"You can't!" she screams. "You can't take back what they fucking did to me! It's your fault, it's all your fucking fault and I hate you for it." Sobs claw their way out of her, her shoulders and body tremble from the force. A good man would hold her and whisper words of love in her ear but I'm not a good man. I'm the devil's kin. I stand here and watch as she tries to hold herself together and not break in front of me. "I... I need to..."

"You need to find an outlet?" She sniffles and nods, her hands gripping the hem of her shirt in a vice like grip. "Fine, I'll give you the outlet that you need but you do it on my terms!" I make sure that my tone shows her I am not going to be swayed on this.

"Okay." I nod and stalk past her to leave but her voice stops me in the doorway. "Where are you going?" I keep my back to her as I answer.

"You need time to process shit, Allison. You're angry and have every right to be but you will not take it out on Amelia. The room is yours, I'll sleep with Mela." I close the door not wanting to hear her reply. Getting her back was supposed to have turned out differently. I knew she would be angry and blame me but I didn't expect her to say she hated me!

I situate Mela on the stool in the kitchen and fix up her breakfast. Kiara and Bishop walk in. When they spot Mela, they both smile brightly at my little girl. Bish ruffles her hair as he heads for the coffee pot, Kiara kisses the top of her head before claiming the stool beside her. Rook and Knight both walk in, neither of them wear a shirt and their hair is a mess.

"What are you making *us* for breakfast?" I playfully scowl at Kiara.

"I'm making Mela fruit salad." Kiara pouts and looks at Mela with sad eyes causing me to roll my own.

"Meelz, Daddy won't feed me and I'm hungry!" Mela gasps and turns her angry little gaze to me.

"Daddy, Aunt Kiara is hungry," she admonishes me. I glare at Kiara who is grinning wide and shoots me a wink. Two can play at this game. I look at Bishop who is leaning back against the counter sipping his coffee.

"Bish, did you know Kiara has been training with Gage?" Kiara's jaw drops and quickly turns to Bishop but he's already glaring at her and squeezing the life out of his mug.

"The fuck is he talking about?" His voice is void of all emotion. Kiara opens her mouth but snaps it closed. Her and Bishop have a rule that they can't lie to each other and it seems the princess is not breaking that deal. "Answer me, Kiara!"

"Don't fucking scream at me, Bishop!"

"Both of you stop cussing in front of Amelia!" Everyone turns to the entryway. Allison stands there in a pair of jean shorts and white shirt that clings to her body like a second skin. Mela spins around so quickly she topples off her stool, the five of us reach for her but Kiara is the one to catch her. She places Mela on her feet and then my girl is shooting across the room. Tears cloud Allison's eyes as she drops to her knees and opens her arms.

"Mommy!" Mela screams as she launches herself at Allison. Ally falls to her ass as she holds our daughter tight against her chest and buries her face in the crook of her neck. No one moves or says a word as we watch the exchange. Amelia hasn't been the same since Allison was taken, she never smiled as bright or laughed freely.

"I missed you so much, baby girl," Allison cries as she peppers kisses all over Mela's face. It hits me, I know what I need to do in order to help Allison heal. I grab Kiara by the hand and haul her out of the room with Bishop hot on my heels. As soon as we are out of ear shot, I release her. Bishop shoves me and gets right in my face.

"You ever fucking touch her like that—"

"Chill, Bish. I just need to talk to her," I plead. I need him to allow her to help me.

"Then fucking talk in there!" Kiara reaches out and pulls him back by his hand. She pushes him against the wall and steps in front of him resting her hands on his chest trying to calm the beast.

"B, look at me." He slowly pulls his heated glare from me to peer down at her, his features changing immediately. His eyes soften and his body relaxes just from looking into her eyes. "If I didn't want to go with him, I would have kicked his ass." I snort but she ignores me. "He needs my help." How she knows that is a mystery to me. Bish grunts and nods, she turns to face me but he wraps his arms around her waist and pulls her back until she is flush against him.

"What do you want?" I don't look at my brother as I answer, I focus on Kiara as I know she is the key to getting me what I want.

"I need you to help me get the shack back up and

running." Her eyes widen in surprise. I feel Bishop's angry glare boring into me but I ignore it. All I need is for Kiara to agree to do this as she is the one that can get Gage to go against my brother. Gage may be our blood but he is loyal to Kiara, not us.

"Like fuck—" She cuts Bishop off.

"Why? Give me one good reason why I should piss off Bishop and potentially get Gage's ass kicked for doing this?" She has every right to be weary, after all I am the one who burnt the shack to the ground under my brother's orders.

"Allison," I breathe. Bishop looks confused but Kiara understands my meaning.

"If Gage gets hurt because of this, I'll kick your fucking ass, King!" I smile and nod.

"Deal, princess."

Chapter Twenty-Three

Allison

Two weeks....

I just exist. I get up and spend the day with Mela doing whatever she likes but I don't leave the estate. King and I don't speak, we pass by each other or I see him when he comes to shower at night before he leaves and sleeps God knows where. He hasn't tried to touch me or sleep with me. He hasn't even fucking looked at me! He hired someone to come and speak with me three times a week. I screamed at the poor woman the first two sessions. On the third session I walked into King's makeshift office ready to yell at her but stopped when I saw Knight sitting there. Having him there relaxed me. We didn't speak about what I went through that session, instead we spoke about him and what he went through with Christine and how it has affected him. My sister was a fucked-up bitch doing what she did to him. He was a fucking kid!

I went myself to the next three sessions, Knight being so open made me feel like it was okay for me to do the same. I don't know if King sent him to be there with me or if he just done it on his own accord. Regardless, I am grateful either way. It's only been three sessions but I find myself looking forward to my one today and ready to open more to Opal. I need to fix myself so I can be better for Mela, she doesn't need to see this darkness that has taken hold of me and corrupted me to be bitter and angry all the time. I head into the library and smile politely at Opal. As I take a seat on the couch opposite her, she has her pad and pen out, ready to get this session started.

"How are you today, Allison?" Her question should be simple but it isn't.

"I know I'm supposed to say I'm doing good but I honestly don't know." Her brown eyes soften behind her thick, black-rimmed glasses, her brown hair pinned back in a bun and she wears a cream-colored pant suit.

"And that is fine, you don't have to know exactly how you are feeling." I nod, not sure how to respond to her. "Would you like to talk about what happened to you or would you—" I cut in before she can finish.

"Yes. If I don't do it now, I don't think I ever will," I whisper.

"Allison, there is no rush or time limit on this. You take all the time you need. We do this at your pace and when you're ready." The fact she hasn't pushed me or ever made me feel like I had to do as she asked has made me feel comfortable with her. I know keeping everything that happened bottled up inside me isn't good. I need to vent even if it's fucking hard.

But I have to know something first. "What I say to you—"

"Stays between us, nothing you tell me will go beyond here unless I think you are a threat to yourself and may self-harm." My eyes widen in shock.

"I wouldn't do that." She smiles and nods.

"I'm just saying, if you were to exhibit signs I would need to let... someone know."

"By *someone*, you mean King?" She sighs but nods regardless. "Thanks for being honest."

"You have my word, nothing said here will go beyond this room. Mr. Murdoch was very specific with that point when he hired me." That shocks me. I thought King would have been getting a detailed report after every session I had with Opal. "When you're ready, please begin." Nodding I take a few deep breaths and try to center myself. I need to get into the right headspace before I can broach the night-mare that was my life.

"I didn't know what was happening. I thought they would just take me and inflict some pain to piss King off, then I'd get to go home. I was so naïve." I twist my hands in my lap to try to control the anxious energy inside me. "Days passed and King never came. Days turned into weeks and I began to lose hope that he would ever come for me. When Koby showed up my hope began to be restored, my will to live returned. She gave me something other than my pain to focus on."

"What did she do that helped you?" I roll my lips over my teeth worried that she will think I'm crazy. "This is a judgment free zone, Allison."

I nod. "She taught me how to fight." Her expression doesn't change, she doesn't even seem put off at my answer.

"Good. How did learning to fight make you feel?" I ponder her question for a moment. I never really thought about it while I was doing it.

"I guess it made me feel... strong, like I could defend myself."

"That's good, Allison. Have you continued that training since you have returned here?" I shake my head and lower my gaze. "May I ask why?"

"King," is my only answer.

"I believe that if this training with Koby has helped you, then you should continue with it. This is about what benefits you and helps you, not anyone else."

"I never thought about it like that." I shrug.

"What else did fighting make you feel?"

"It made me feel like I would never be at their mercy again. If they came back, I would be able to put up a fight. I guess, I feel like now that I know some basic moves that I could at least fight them off. I lost a part of myself there... They stole something from me that I will never get back." Tears threaten to spill and I try to fight them back. I don't want to cry, I want to move past this but it's fucking hard. Each night I lay in bed and wonder if King will come and claim me. I know it sounds pathetic, but the truth is I need him to wash away the bad and make me remember what it was like to be worshiped and not used.

"What do you mean at their mercy?"

"They would come into the room I was held in and... rape me." I watch her waiting to see the pity in her eyes but it doesn't come.

"I understand." I grind my teeth, I'm so sick of hearing people fucking say that!

"No, you don't. How could you know what it was like to be raped by over a dozen men... Have them tear you open front and back and then laugh at the destruction they caused?" She lifts her glasses and places them on the top of her head.

"I understand because I have been where you are. Did you think Mr. Murdoch just chose any therapist?" She shakes her head at me. "I was sold into a sex trafficking ring when I was four years old. Anthony Bennett saved my life and set me free at the age of seventeen. I owe my life to that man and all he asked of me in return is that I make something of myself and not allow my past to define my future. I was raped more times than I can count. I don't even remember their faces because there were just that many. Now, can we move on and assume from here on out that I do know what I'm talking about?" I slouch back against the couch thoroughly chastised and feeling like shit. Looking at her you would never think that she suffered such a horrific ordeal.

"I'm sorry," I mumble.

"Don't be. I'm not my past, Allison, and nor are you. May I be frank with you for a moment?"

I nod my head. "Yeah, go for it."

"You have two choices. One, you can allow those sons of bitches to win and keep wallowing in the darkness and letting it destroy you daily. Two, you can find something that gives you power and strength and makes you feel alive. Use that to push past your nightmares and reclaim who you are now. You will never go back to being the old Allison, so you need to learn to adapt and accept the new *you*."

She's right. Everything she just said is exactly what I needed to hear. I know what I have to do now. I'll make this work because I want to be better for Mela and she needs me to be better. I won't allow her to see me crumble and break apart because of some sick twisted assholes who thought they could use my body to break her father.

One month...

Koby and I train every day. Dimitri sits out back and watches but never joins in. Mela has come out a few times and watched but when King found out I was allowing her to train with Koby and I, he lost his shit. That was the first time he had spoken to me in weeks. He still doesn't sleep in the bed with me. He has had a bed moved into Mela's room. I hate the space between us but I don't know how to close it. When Koby lands a right hook to my jaw, I cry out and stumble back a step. I rub the spot and glare at her. She scowls at me, her long blonde hair is in a high ponytail. She wears a blacks sports bra that show off her perfect tits, gray tights that show off her toned ass. Her body is a work of art.

"You're distracted!" she snaps.

"I have a lot on my mind," I defend. Koby is a cold bitch, she doesn't care for excuses.

"I don't give a shit. I told you that if I was to train you that you come here each day and focus, not waste my fucking time." I throw my hands in the air.

"Excuse me for not being a fucking robot like you!" Koby gets right in my face.

"Me being like this has kept me alive. I didn't have a rich-ass baby daddy to hide out with." I shove her back and clock her across the jaw. She recovers quickly and tackles me to the grass. We grapple for control until Dimitri begins to scream. Koby freezes on top of me and we both turn to D who is as pale as a ghost. Before either of us can ask if he's okay, Koby is shoved from atop me and I'm yanked to my feet. An arm snakes around my waist and hauls me against his chest. My back burns with the feeling of him pressed against me. Koby stands and glares at King over my head. She opens her mouth to shout at him but then Knight storms over to her and blocks her view. His back rises and falls with his rapid pants, his fists are clenched at his sides.

"Don't ever fucking touch her like that again!" My eyes widen in shock at Knight's defense of me.

"Eat shit, asshole. She knew it was coming when she blind shotted me." It's true, I knew she would whoop my ass.

"Do it again and I'll make you regret it, you Russian whore." I gasp.

"Knight! That's enough," I growl. Koby may be a bitch but she's my friend and doesn't deserve to be spoken to like that. Koby ignores my protest as her and Knight continue to argue. I struggle in King's hold but he won't release me. "Let me go!" I snap at the overbearing asshole. He ignores me for weeks and then decides he wants to come play hero? I don't think so.

"You're done training for the day," is all he says before he grabs my hand and pulls me after him.

Chapter Twenty-Four

King

I white knuckle the steering wheel and keep my gaze ahead. If I look over at her my cock will void all rational thought and I'll just pull the car over and fuck her. She looks like a fucking snack in her tiny-ass, skin-tight black shorts and white sports bra. She fought me the whole way to the car but I refused to give into her demands. I'm tired of being away from her. Opal says she has made huge progress in such a short time and that training with Koby has really helped her. I've done as she asked and left Allison be to come to terms with things in her own time, but I'm done waiting. I need my girl back!

We pull into the carpark of the new industrial building I had built. It doesn't look like much, just a plain old factory but it's the inside that will sell this to her. I slam the car in park and get out. I expect to have to drag her in but I'm pleasantly surprised to see her follow my lead. I round the car and grip her hand in mine. She doesn't protest or say a word as I lead her toward the door. My nerves are frayed. I'm beginning to worry I've made a huge mistake and I'm going to put her ten steps back. I rap my knuckles against the door and wait. I look down at Allison but her face is void of all emotion, I'm starting to fucking hate that Koby bitch. Her cold detached ways are starting to rub off on my girl and I don't fucking like it. I want the old Ally back. The door opens and Gage stands there with a smile on his face as he waves us in. Allison follows after me but stops in her tracks.

I watch as she takes everything in—the ring in the middle, all the boxing bags and gym equipment that surround us. I made sure to have everything state of the art brought in for her. I didn't want her training in some grungy piece of shit place. The top floor is a mask for what really happens. Beneath us in the basement is where Gage will run our underground fight ring again. Bishop is pissed about it but it only took Kiara sucking his cock for him to change his mind.

"What is this?" Her voice is barely above a whisper and filled with awe. I release her hand and cup her face looking into her eyes.

"No more home training for you. You want to train and learn to fight, then you do it here." Her mouth opens and closes and I prepare myself for her to fight me on this.

"What about Koby? Can she train here as well?" I want to roll my eyes and say *fuck no* but instead I find myself saying,

"If that's what you want." A small shy smile graces her angelic face.

"Why did you do this?" She doesn't even pretend to act like she doesn't know I did all of this for her and that is one of the reasons I love her, she never minces her words.

"Because, if fighting is what makes you happy, then I want you trained by the best." I breath in through my nose and grit out through clenched teeth. It fucking hurts my ego to admit this. "Gage is the best and he will train you, so will Kiara." Her eyes widen and her mouth opens slightly.

"You're going to let Gage train me?" Her eyes dart to the fucker in question who stands a few feet away with his arms crossed over his chest and a shit eating grin on his face. He shoots her a wink and it has me growling, which just causes him to laugh. How the fuck is he related to me?

"If *him* training you means you will be safe and learn the right way, then yes. Mark my words though, Allison, you will not be entering the under-ground fight ring." Her eyes harden at the edges.

"Why the fuck not?" I release my hold on her and step back. I run my gaze over her and smile wickedly, my cock is rock hard and dying to be deep inside her cunt.

"You'll get your fight, but when I say you are ready."

I stayed with Allison as she trained for a couple hours with Gage. I hated watching him with his hands on her. I wanted to rip his arms from his body and beat him with them. I saw her tense the first couple of times he touched her to correct her stance or how to hold her fists, but after a while she got used to it. I hate to admit it but Gage is good with her. He makes sure she can see where his hands are at all times, announces when he is showing her a move from behind so it doesn't trigger her in any way. She was excited that he said he would see her first thing in the morning. It warmed my heart when she changed the time of their training to later so she could continue to do her breakfast routine with Mela.

We ride home in silence. It's not awkward or filled with tension. Well, it is definitely filled with sexual tension but I'm not sure if that's just me. By the time I pull into the drive the sun has set. After I park we climb out and as we walk to the door, this time she reaches out and interlaces her fingers with mine. I try not to let my shock show as we walk through the door and instead of joining the others in the living room, I lead her up the stairs. I don't need my fucking brothers eye fucking her in *that* outfit. As we enter my room, I close the door behind us and release her hand. She nibbles on her lip and fidgets with her hair. I hate that she feels awkward around me.

"I'm gonna take a shower. I won't be long and then you can have it." I don't wait for her reply as I head into the bathroom and turn the faucet of the shower on, then make quick work of stripping off and climbing in. The hot water relaxes my muscles but it does nothing to soothe my rock hard cock. I refuse to bring myself pleasure until it's with Allison. I want her to be the one to make me come. I lean my head back and allow the water to cover my face. My eyes snap open when I feel someone else enter the shower. Water beats down on me and I have to keep blinking rapidly to make sure my eyes aren't playing tricks on me. Allison stands before me naked, her blue eyes are filled with lust as she runs her gaze over my naked chest. When she reaches my aching cock, her tongue darts out to moisten her lips, making me groan.

She closes the space between us and I remain still

keeping my eyes on hers as she runs her hands down my chest. I shiver under her touch. She traces the lines of my abs and I fight the urge to reach out and tweak her nipple when I see them begin to harden. A hiss escapes me when she runs a single finger down the length of my cock—just one small touch from her and already I want to come. She steps back and exits the shower. I slam my eyes closed and mentally berate myself for getting carried away.

"I need you to not touch me." My eyes fly open. She stands in front of me again with a towel. She drops it to the floor and kneels in front of me. Her blue eyes remain on me as she reaches out and grips my cock in her tiny hand causing me to buck in surprise. "Okay?" For a moment I can't even think straight until her question from a moment ago registers. I lock my arms behind my back and nod, making a relieved sigh escape her. I watch transfixed as she uses both hands to stroke me. I moan, fuck it feels so good having her hands on me again. When a drop of pre cum coats the top of my cock she leans forward and darts her tongue out to taste it.

"Fuck!" I moan, she doesn't stop. She sucks my cock as far as she can into the back of her throat, gagging around it but fuck the sight and sound of it has me digging my nails into my ass to fight not to touch her. She bobs up and down on my cock, unable to fit me all the way in, so she uses her hands to stroke me. I want to close my eyes and savor the moment but I'm too transfixed on how fucking beautiful she looks on her knees. My girl sucks cock like a hoover. I can feel my balls tightening and know I won't last much longer. I don't want to come down her throat. "Baby?" Her blue eyes meet mine and I groan, my cock looks so fucking good in her mouth.

"Hmmm?" Is her only response as she refuses to let my cock go.

"Can I fuck you?" She releases my cock and licks her lips. "I promise I will do whatever you say or stop whenever—"

"I'm on top. I'm in control." Her stern voice tells me she needs this. I nod my head like an idiot and follow her out of the shower like a puppy. She stands beside the bed with water droplets cascading down her body, my mouth waters begging me to taste her. "Lay down—" I cut off her demand when I grip her face and smash my lips against hers, the taste of her on my tongue has me moaning. I don't deepen the kiss, I pull back and rest my forehead against hers.

"I want this. I want you more than anything, baby, but I won't be a business transaction. I'll give you whatever you need but the moment you go somewhere else in that pretty little mind of yours, we stop." Her eyes mist with tears.

"H-how did you know?" She has no idea that I have been watching her since the moment she came back. I even wait till she's asleep and sneak in here just to stare at her. I see her disappear inside her own mind and it kills me that I can't go with her. I want to protect her but I can't do that. I wish I could crawl inside her mind and hold her hand through it all but she needs to do this on her own. I won't have my strong, independent college girl rely on me when she can do this on her own. The monster inside me wants her to need me and rely on me, but the rational side of my brain knows that if I did that I would lose the Allison I know and love.

"I see it. When you think no one is looking, you disappear inside that pretty little head of yours. If you want me to be your escape and keep you grounded, I can do that but you need to be present, with me." Tears spill down her cheeks. I lean down and lick them, then run my tongue along the column of her neck and relish in the shudder that rolls through her. "I want to taste these tits, baby," I breath out as I cup them. She shudders against me as I run the pad of my thumb over her pebbled nipple.

"I'm scared," she whispers. I choose to ignore that comment as I bend down and capture her nipple. She cries out and thrusts her tit further into my mouth. I slowly trace my hands around her waist, giving her time to pull back if she needs to. She thinks she needs to be in control of this but she won't admit it to herself that she likes it when I take charge and fuck her how I want. She has been through hell and thinks it makes her weak if she bends to my will, but this woman is anything but meek and weak. She is a fucking force. I tighten my hold on her and pull her against me. She runs her fingers through my hair and tugs on the strands when I bite down on her nipple. "Fuck, King," she moans.

I release her nipple and switch to other side paying it the same amount of attention. My cock is leaking pre cum and is so fucking hard it actually pains me. I release her nipple and pepper kisses down her stomach as I drop to my knees in front of her. Her blue eyes are wide and filled with lust. I grip her thigh and throw it over my shoulder before gripping her ass in both my hands and pulling her pussy against my face. I inhale her intoxicating scent and groan, fuck her pussy smells good and I know it tastes even better. She's quivering in my hold as I dart my tongue out and swipe it up her slit. She screams out in pleasure, so I continue to lick up and down her slit, always missing her clit. It's driving her wild and I fucking love it. She grips my hair and tries to pull my head where she wants it but I one up her. I bury my tongue inside her tight wet cunt and relish in her scream.

"Oh my God. Tongue fuck my dirty pussy, King. Make me come all over your fucking face!" Her dirty talk has me stunned for a moment, she really has changed and fuck me if it doesn't turn me the fuck on. I do as she says and continue to fuck her with my tongue. She rides my face like a cowgirl. "It's not enough, finger fuck me and suck my clit so I come all over your fucking face... Now!"

Chapter Twenty-Five

Allison

As soon as he pushes two fingers inside my greedy cunt and sucks my clit into his mouth, I know I won't last long. I want to draw this out and bask in the moment of not being able to think and only feel but he's fucking me too good with his mouth and I want his cock buried so deep inside me that I won't know where he begins and I end. I feel my orgasm cresting. I tug on his hair and ride his fingers faster, I need this orgasm more than I need my next breath. I need him to make sex a beautiful and good thing for me again, not something dirty and tainted.

"Oh God, just like that, baby. Make me come and then fuck me," I moan out. Not a second later I come so fucking hard black spots dance in the corners of my eyes and my knees give out but King tightens his hold on me. He slowly stands to his feet. I expect him to kiss me but instead he holds his two fingers out and tells me,

"Suck your cum off them and tell me how good your cunt tastes." My pussy clenches at his words. I open my mouth and moan at the taste when he inserts his fingers. I swirl my tongue around his digits and love the way his pupils widen. "Get on the bed and open your legs so I can see *my* pussy." He yanks his fingers out and I do as he says, climbing on the bed and rolling onto my back. I try to keep the dark thoughts from my mind but when he nestles between my legs fear begins to take over and I start to get short of breath. "Fuck," he snaps before leaning down and kissing me. For a moment I lay here frozen with fear, until he cups my face and pulls back. We're nose to nose just gazing into each other's eyes. "Stay with me, baby. Let me make love to you and show you without words how much I love you." Tears leak from the corners of my eyes as I nod. He leans back and slowly lines his angry red cock up with my entrance. He keeps his eyes on me as he slowly pushes forward, a moan slipping out of me at the feeling of having him inside me. I'm grateful that I have had an IUD for a couple years now—if I didn't have it, I would hate to think of what might have happened whilst I was being held.

"Just do it," I grit out. King smirks and obeys my command. He slams inside me and we both cry out in pleasure.

"Baby, I need to fuck you fast. I won't last long but I promise I'll make it up to you."

"Fuck me, make me come on your cock and then you can fuck me all night long." My words have his eyes glazing over. He lifts my legs and places them over his shoulders, leans forward and rests his hands either side of me. I'm folded up like a staple. He thrusts inside me and holy fuck, it is the perfect angle. He is relentless in how fast and hard he fucks me. I scream out in pleasure, my orgasm is cresting again and I know it is going to knock the air from my lungs. "King, don't fucking stop, I'm about to come," I shout.

"Come with me, baby. I'm right there. Come all over my fucking cock!" A moment later we both come screaming the other's name. I feel his hot jets of cum deep inside me and the feeling of having him so deep inside my body has me clenching his cock. He moans at the feeling, then I shove him back. He jumps off me and scurries off the bed in fright. I follow after him, his shocked and worried gaze still on me as I drop to my knees in front of him and suck his cock. "Oh fuck, Ally, baby." I moan at the taste of him and suck his cock clean. Once I have licked every drop, I release his cock and sit back on my haunches staring up at him. I wipe my thumb across my lips and suck the cum off it moaning.

"I love the taste of my cum mixed with yours. Let's get cleaned up and see our daughter, then I need you to fuck me until I pass out," I say as I climb to my feet. His eyes are wide and his jaw slightly ajar. I smile and head into the bathroom to clean up.

Four weeks....

King and I have been sharing his–*our*–room, as he insists I call it, for the past month. I still see Opal three times a week. Between her, training with Gage and King helping me overcome my fears of sex, I feel like... I'm okay. Some days are harder than others. If one of the guys brush past me from behind I still jump or scream. None of them make a big deal out of it or even comment. They used to say sorry all the time but I asked them to stop. I told them all over dinner one night that I just want to be treated normal and not like a broken doll. That night King fucked me so good and hard because he said he was proud of me. I spend my mornings with Mela and then head to the gym to train. Kiara and the twins have gone back to school. Bishop has laid down the law and told them they have to clear out their dorms and be back by the end of the week. He doesn't want them away whilst a war is going on between all the families. Tony, Kiara's father, is supposed to be flying in this week.

"Keep your guard up and make sure to stay out of your head!" Gage pins me with a disapproving glare. I smile sheepishly and do as he asks. I don't know why he changed our time to evening today, we never train this late and I hate that I'm missing putting Mela to bed. "Go with the left, right combo and then switch it up with a shin kick." I follow his instructions. He smiles proudly down at me when I execute his order. He drops the pads from his hands and claps me on the shoulder. I don't know what it is about Gage but for some reason I don't fear his touch. It's almost like he knows what I am going through and is aware of how to handle me. "You did good. Take the weekend off and I'll see you Monday." I furrow my brow in confusion and watch as he jumps over the ropes and makes his way toward the locker rooms.

"Gage!" I shout, he doesn't stop or turn around. I squeal in fright when I hear someone jump into the ring behind me, spin around and come to stop. My eyes widen in surprise, King stands there in a pair of black shorts and nothing else. His hands are taped like he is ready to fight. "What are you doing?" He smiles. God he looks so good when he smiles like that.

"I told you, when you were ready, I would let you fight and from what I hear from Gage, you are." My brows raise as I stare at him like he has lost his fucking mind.

"I'm not fighting *you*!" I admonish. He shrugs his shoulders and begins to jump around the ring, cracking his neck side to side.

"You once said you hated me—"

"I didn't mean it!" He ignores me and carries on.

"I saw the look in your eyes, baby. You meant it at the time and I know you wanted to inflict as much pain on me as you could. Now is your chance." He holds his arms out wide as I shake my head vigorously.

"King, no. I won't fight you—"

"You can and you will." The determination in his voice pisses me off.

"Why the fuck would you want me to hurt you?"

"Do this and you will get the best gift I could ever offer you." I snort.

"I get to fuck you every night so it's not a new gift." He groans and I laugh when tries to adjust his hardening cock.

"Don't say shit like that when you're practically fucking naked!" I scoff. I'm wearing tights and a sports bra, he is so over dramatic! "Fight me and find out," he taunts.

"There is nothing in this world that I want enough to fight you—"

"Fight me and I'll give you the papers to legally adopt Amelia and become her mother in the eyes of the law." I freeze, everything inside me stills. I hear nothing but the pounding of my heart in my ears. Tears cloud my vision as King makes his way toward me. I hold my hands flat against his chest to stop his movement. He knocks my hands away and cups my face between his hands. Tears flow freely down my face, his eyes soften as they meet my gaze. "You are already her mother, Allison. I just want it on paper so that no one will ever be able to take her from you like you feared."

I smack his hands away and launch myself at him. He catches me as I wrap my legs around his waist and capture his lips in a heated kiss. My nipples harden and scrape against his bare chest, my pussy slick with need. He breaks our kiss and I growl in frustration which only causes him to chuckle. "So, is that a yes to fighting me?" I pretend to ponder his answer for a moment before struggling in his hold. He releases me and I immediately drop to my knees.

His eyes track my every move as I grip the waistband of his shorts and pull them down. The gym is empty so I know we won't be caught. His cock is already hard and my mouth waters at the sight of it. I don't draw it out, but grip his cock and line it up with my mouth. He throws his head back and moans. I bob up and down on his cock, stroking the remainder of him that I can't fit. I moan at the taste of his pre cum on my tongue.

I keep sucking him nice and deep. I cup his balls in the palm of my free hand, then he reaches down and grips my hair holding me in place as he quickens his pace. I can feel his cock getting bigger in my mouth, I know he is so close and I wait right up till the last second before pulling back. His mouth drops open in shock, his eyes clouded with lust.

"What the fuck, baby. I was about to come!" I smile sweetly at him and run the tips of my fingers over my nipples and moan. His eyes spark with lust. His tongue darts out to moisten his lips as I roll my nipples between my fingers and moan. "Fuck, baby, let me—"

"No!" His eyes blaze and I smile as I grip my sports bra and pull it over my head. My tits feel so heavy from how horny I am. I grip the waistband of my tights and slide them down my legs. I pick my panties up and I can feel how soaked they are. I ball them up and chuck them at him. He catches them and immediately brings them to his nose, eyes closing as he inhales my scent and moans.

"Fuck, your pussy smells so good, baby. Let me eat it."

"No, you get to watch until you admit I won this fight." His eyes snap open as I sink to the floor of the ring. I rest back against the ropes and spread my legs wide open so he has a good view of my dripping cunt. He bites his bottom lip as I trail my hand down my stomach and run a finger through my slick folds. I swirl it around my clit and moan as my hips buck forward from the feeling. King moves forward but I pin him with a look that has him halting. I insert a finger inside my pussy and moan, I'm so fucking wet that I slide in with no resistance. "Fuck, oh God," I moan as I start to pump in and out of my pussy.

"Fuck, Allison. Let me fuck you!" I hold his gaze.

"My pussy feels so tight, baby, and it's so fucking wet." He groans and scrubs a hand down his face as I continue to finger fuck my pussy, while tweaking my nipple in my other hand. I pull my finger out and bring it to my mouth, his eyes burning with lust as he watches me suck my digit clean.

"Jesus! Allison, you're fighting fucking dirty." I reach down and circle my clit as I hold his gaze and moan his name. "Jesus Christ. Fine, you win. Now turn the fuck around cause I'm going to destroy my fucking pussy for that little stunt!" I smile triumphantly and do as he says. I shiver when he nudges my legs apart and lines his cock up with my greedy cunt. He doesn't ease into it gently, he slams inside me in one fluid move. I scream out. He grips my ponytail and pulls my hair so my back is flush with his chest. I grind down on his cock and relish in his moan. "You like that, baby?"

"Fuck, yes!"

"You like my cock deep in your greedy little cunt?" I moan as he thrusts his hips inside me, his cock is the most fucking glorious gift in the world.

"Yessss," I cry out as he continues to fuck me.

"Fuck yes, I can feel your pussy squeezing my cock. Fucking come all over it and then get on your knees like the dirty girl you are and suck it fucking clean!" His words are my undoing. I scream out my release and come all over his fucking cock just like he ordered me to. He doesn't wait for the shocks of my orgasm to reside. He pulls out of me and climbs to his feet. He slaps his dick across my face a couple of times, smearing my cum over me before finally shoving it in my mouth and making me gag. "Fuck yes. I love it when you choke on my cock!" I moan around his girth and keep my hands behind my back and let him set the pace. He fucks my face so fucking good that I have spit dripping down my naked chest. My pussy is aching with need. "Suck it, baby. I'm about to come!" I do as he asks and suck him as deep as I can before jets of his cum slide down my throat.

Chapter Twenty-Six

King

One week later.

I keep my hands on Allison's hips as she stands in front of Mike and Donny, both of them have lost weight. Their faces are gaunt and their skin is pale. They have been fed and watered enough to keep them alive, but they still wear the same soiled clothes from when we took them months ago. We aren't Savages, we do hose them off every couple of days. Can't have our guests sitting in their shit for weeks. Bishop, Gage, Mav and Luka stand behind us. The twins and Kiara are back at the house with Mela.

"You don't have to do this, baby," I whisper. She shakes her head but keeps her gaze on the two dead men walking, each strapped to a chair.

"I need to do this. They fucking deserve it." She pulls out of my hold and moves to stand between the two assholes. She reaches out and pulls the gags from their mouths. They both eye her wearily. Allison exudes confidence but I know her, she is scared and I can't blame her. She is standing before the two men who orchestrated her worst nightmare.

"Was it worth it?" Her voice is firm and doesn't waiver which makes me proud.

"Was, what?" Donny rasps, his lips are dry and chapped and I love the look of death on him. I can smell it in this room, they don't have long before their organs fail them.

"Raping me?" I flinch, and I hear the growls from the four behind and know they hate hearing what she went through. My brothers love Allison. They were all on board and helped me get the adoption together for Mela. Allison signed the papers as soon as we got home from the gym that night, she is legally and officially Mela's mother. "Don't be scared... King won't hurt you." Both Donny and Mikey swing their gazes to me. I step back and lean against the wall between Bishop and Gage crossing my arms over my chest.

"It wasn't personal—" She cuts Mikey off.

"It was just business?" she supplies. Mikey, the stupid fuck, smiles and nods. I furrow my brow in suspicion as she reaches into the waistband of her jeans and pulls out a dagger. Before anyone can prepare for what is about to happen, she stabs the dagger into Mickey's cock. He screams out in horrific pain. I cup my cock on instinct and watch as Bishop and Gage do the same.

"You fucking bitch!" Mikey screams. I step forward ready to beat his ass but Allison's laughter has me halting.

She twists the dagger causing him to scream out, tears leaking from his eyes.

"Oh, don't be silly. From where I'm standing, you're the bitch now! I get to do whatever the fuck I want to you both and there isn't a fucking thing you can do about it. You sick fucks broke into my home and tried to take me and my daughter." Donny's brow furrows causing Allison to laugh again. She yanks the dagger from Mikey's cock and without warning, stabs it into Donny's, the fucker screams just as loud. "I saw you asshole's pull up. I hid her. There was no fucking way you sick pigs would ever lay a hand on my daughter." She yanks the dagger out again and then spins to face us, none of us move or speak as we stare at her. She has the same blood thirsty look in her eyes that I get when I'm down here. "You said you would get me whatever I want and help me do whatever I want, right?" I nod like an idiot, at a loss as to how to answer. "Good. I need a blow torch and a bat wrapped in barbwire." She turns but pauses and looks back over her shoulder. "Could you boy's help me get them on their hands and knees first, please?"

I fucking love this woman!

Bishop and Gage keep shooting Allison side glances as we eat dinner. It's starting to piss me off! I look beside me and see Mela has finished her dinner. She even ate her veggies like her mother ordered. I whisper in her ear that she can go play in her room. She smiles and jumps from her seat and races up the stairs. I shoot Luka a look from across the room. He nods and follows after her. There are still two families vying for us, so until we take them out, we have a full security team in and around the house. I pin both Bishop and Gage with a glare and snap.

"Why the fuck are you two looking at her like that?" Bishop scoffs. Gage rolls his eyes and drops his fork to his plate.

"How the fuck can she sit there and eat after what she did?" Allison just chuckles and continues to eat her chicken.

"What'd she do?"

"Shut up Rook!" I snap.

"I shoved a barbwire baseball up the asses of the men that raped me and then used a blow torch to burn their tiny cocks and made them eat it before they died." Rook, Knight and Kiara gape at Allison's answer. I puff my chest out like a proud motherfucker, my baby had them fucking screaming and begging for death. Bishop even offered her a job working for the family as our *information expert*. I declined but she fucking accepted and skipped out of the bunker like nothing happened.

"Uh, yeah, nope. I'm not even going to ask." Allison laughs at Rook's response. Pretty soon everyone joins in and laughs along with her.

I sit here and gaze around the table at my family. A few months ago, I never thought this would happen. I had planned to torment Allison and make her pay for hiding my daughter but instead, I fell in love with the woman who saved my child and raised her without asking for a fucking cent. I am in awe of Allison daily. Even now, when we have all the money we could need at our fingertips, she still won't allow me to throw Mela a lavish party for her fifth birthday. This woman is going to keep me humble for the rest of my life. I pull out my phone and send a text to Luka. Within a few minutes, Mela comes racing down the stairs and straight into the dining room, heading straight for Allison.

"Mommy?" Allison reaches out and strokes her cheek.

"Yeah, baby?"

"Daddy and me got to ask you something special." I stand from my seat and move around to the other side of Allison where Mela stands, then drop to one knee beside my daughter. Allison's hand comes up to cover her mouth as she gasps, tears filling her blue eyes.

"Fate doesn't always get things right in my world but she did this time. You're perfect. You challenge me at every turn, you love me even when I don't deserve it. You're the best mother to our daughter and I want forever with you. Will you marry *us*?" Before she can answer, Mela cuts in.

"You have to say yes. Daddy says if you don't, he's gonna spank you, Mommy!" I groan and the others laugh. Allison does as well. Mela pulls out the ring from her pocket and holds it out to Allison, it's a simple diamond band with a red ruby in the center of it. I grab it from Mela and slip it on her finger as tears leak from her eyes.

"She didn't say yes!" I snap my gaze to Rook and glare at the fucker. Allison grips my face and turns me back to her.

"Yes, in this life and every other life, my answer will always be yes!"

Epilogue

King

Later that night.

I've just put Mela to bed when I can hear shouts coming from down the hall by Knight's room. I head to his room to tell him to shut up but pause when I see, Rook, Gage and Bishop in there with him.

"Shut the fucking door behind you!" I do as Bishop orders and stand here with my brothers at a loss at to what the fuck has happened.

"Someone want to fill me in?" I ask.

"Your baby momma's Russian friend is a fucking spy." I glare at Gage.

"Watch your fucking mouth when you speak about my fiancée!" The threat in my voice is clear.

"He's not lying. Koby isn't who she says she is." I hold Knight's gaze.

"Someone want to explain how the fuck you know this or are we just gonna stand here all night and hold each other's cocks?" Rook shudders and shakes his head.

"Tell him!" Knight snaps. I follow his gaze to Rook who seems pissed off at his twin.

"You're a fucking snitch, brother," Rook seethes but Knight just shrugs it off. Whatever Rook knows has Knight wound up. I may be the one who can inflict pain and don't bat an eye but Knight, he craves it like he needs it to survive. Whatever Christine did to him has him fucked up and going down a dark fucking path that I don't know if he can come back from.

"I got a text," Rook grits out. I quirk a brow.

"From who?" I'm getting tired of this already, getting information from the twins is like pulling fucking teeth!

"Our sister." That has my full attention. I look to Bishop who nods, confirming Rook's story.

"And what did she say?"

"Her name isn't Koby, King. Her real name is Anya Volkov. Her and her kid brother Dimitri are the children of Russian Bratva Pakhan, Vladimir Volkov. They aren't just some random Russians in New York, they are the heirs to the Russian mob!"

Click the link to read Knight's story,
Tortured By The Knight

THANK YOU!

Are you still with me?
Did you enjoy the ride?
Don't hate me for the cliff hanger, I swear the wait will be worth it.
I hope you fell in love with King the same way I did, he and Ally went through some shit and man did they fight their way back to each other.
Thank you for coming on this wild ride and loving these boys and girls as much as I do.

Please if you loved the book leave a review on **Amazon, Bookbub** or **Goodreads**, it would mean a lot to hear your feedback.

The third book in the series is Tortured By The Knight

Blurb

Knight

Pain.
Darkness.
That's what my life is. Always has been.

Koby is the opposite.
Light and redemption.

She can see through to my tortured soul, see into the depths, the parts that want to torture her, remove the light from her eyes. Break her until she's nothing just like me.

She thinks she can save me. Like there is something left to be salvaged.

She has no idea I'm not the white knight in her story, there is no happily ever after for us.

Koby

He was born to hate me.
I was born to hate him.
We are the modern-day Romeo and Juliet, both of us born into waring families.

I see the pain, darkness behind his eyes.

Will his darkness snuff out the light of my soul?
Or can I be the brightness that he so desperately needs?

I'm no princess, but right now I need to be saved, and I've just found my Knight.

ALSO BY SAMANTHA BARRETT

Paranormal Romance

The Dream Series

The Dream Trilogy

A Beautiful Dream

A Twisted Fate

A Beautiful Nightmare

Redemption

Anarchy

Brutal Savages

Savage Lies

Brutal Truth

Savage Beast

Brutal Beauty

Mafia Romance

Murdoch Mafia Series

Played By The Bishop

Tormented By The King

Tortured By The Knight

Tempted By The Queen

Turned By The Pawn

Ruined By The Rook

<u>Memento Mori Series</u>

Reign Of Royal

BBS

IHLC

DBHA

<u>Fairytales With A Twist</u>

Condemned Beast

Sports Romance

<u>Playing For Keeps</u>

<u>Duet</u>

Offside

Touchdown

End Game

Hail Mary

Blindside

RH Sports

Hate Us Like You Mean It

Love Me Like You Mean It

ACKNOWLEDGMENTS

First off,

Thank you first and foremost to my beta team, ARC team and PA for loving Bishop and pushing me to write King faster. Your love for each of these boys keeps me pushing to smash out each of these books and deliver the best story I can.

My Mum, Dad and bonus Dad, thank you for supporting me through this journey as an author and continuing to push me to chase my dreams.

My baby daddy, my ride or die, my husband. I love you but I may just love your dick the most.

My babies, you are my everything, my reason, my heart beat and my life. I love you both beyond measure.

Last but not least, my readers.

Thank you all so much for following me along this journey and taking a leap of faith by reading one of my books. Your support means the world to me, without it I wouldn't be able to live out my dream of being an author!

Until next time my loves,
Sam Xxx

ABOUT THE AUTHOR

Samantha Barrett is a dark romance, PNR author who loves to write out-of-the-box stories. She is originally from the land of the long white cloud, New Zealand. She is totally fluking her way through this whole author gig, if she isn't writing you can find her kicking back with her kids and husband with a bag of chips and a glass of wine in her hand. Sam loves Twilight and is a TWIHARD proudly.